Coraline

A Visual Companion

STEPHEN JONES

WILLIAM MORROW
An Imprint of HarperCollinsPublishers

FIRST EDITION

Designed by Joel Avirom and Jason Snyder

Library of Congress Cataloging-in-Publication Data has been applied for.

ISBN 978-0-06-170422-2

09 10 11 12 13   ov/qw   10 9 8 7 6 5 4 3 2 1

Contents

Those of us who write stories sometimes nurse fantasies that our stories will out-live us—the two things you leave behind you that change the world are children and art, as Stephen Sondheim pointed out in *Sunday in the Park with George*, and art for children is special. *Coraline* was art I made for my daughters, to amuse and frighten and excite and entertain them.

It was a story I loved telling, although I felt a little guilty that it took me so long to finish.

I was told a few times that it was too dark a story for children, but children did not, on the whole, seem to think so. It was definitely, I learned soon, too dark for some adults, which is why there is an edition for adults that warns them how scary it is on the front cover.

Sometimes you get lucky. You make art that does more than you hoped it would.

I had hoped to write a book that would amuse my daughters, and I like the idea that a few children would read it and remember it, would perhaps go and look for it when they, in their turn, had grown up, would hunt down dusty old secondhand copies and force them on their own children in their turn.

I am proud of *Coraline*. Her story is told in many languages. (She's *Koralina* in Eastern Europe. I am told that in China the title of her book translates as *Coraline Fights the Button-eyed Witch*.) She has scared

Danish journalists and disturbed German publishers. She has received many awards, most of which I have accepted on her behalf (I wasn't able to accept the one from the children of Louisiana. Hurricane Katrina came, and the awards ceremony was canceled). She's been onstage, she's becoming a musical, and now she's the star of her own film.

I don't think it would go to her head. If she knew about it, I doubt she'd give it a second thought, not when there are doors she has never been through, new worlds to explore, animals and people to meet.

I get letters about her all the time, asking whether we will see her again, most of them asking for another story with Coraline Jones in it. I do not want to write a story about Coraline that isn't as good as *Coraline*, so until I find a story that's better than the one with the door, and the other mother, you'll just have to content your-self with imagining.

And with a musical. And with a movie. And with a graphic novel. And with this book, which tells you about the journeys that Coraline has taken so far.

You should be grateful to Steve Jones, who makes things happen with aplomb and verve, and made this book happen when all the odds were against it. And even if you aren't grateful, let me assure you that I am.

Neil Gaiman
June 2008

1
The Book

Fairy tales are more than true;
not because they tell us that dragons exist,
but because they tell us that dragons can be beaten.

— G. K. CHESTERTON

Many years ago, in a house not far from the sea, a writer made up a bedtime story for his young daughter.

That's because that is what writers do.

This particular writer's name was Neil, and the little girl was called Holly.

The years passed, as years are wont to do, and the story was still not finished.

By now the family lived in another country—many hundreds of miles away from where the story was first begun.

Then another little girl came along, and her name was Maddy.

In time, she also wanted to hear a bedtime story. So the writer decided to finish the tale that he had started all those years earlier for the other daughter.

And when, eventually, he did finally come to the end of his story, it was only then that the writer went looking for someone to publish it . . .

OPPOSITE

Coraline scowls when her mother refuses to buy
her a pair of colorful gloves in the sale.

Neil Gaiman was born in the market town of Portchester, Southeast England, in 1960. Five years later, his family moved into an old manor house with ten acres of ground in the East Sussex town of East Grinstead (he's on the town's Hall of Fame Web site).

As a youngster, Gaiman grew up reading the works of C. S. Lewis, Lord Dunsany, G. K. Chesterton, J. R. R. Tolkien, Ursula K. Le Guin, and Michael Moorcock. After leaving school, he became a journalist, contributing articles, interviews, and reviews to a wide variety of newspapers and magazines. He sold his first professional story in 1984, along with a biography of 1980s pop idols Duran Duran.

"That's the kind of thing you do when you're a twenty-two-year-old journalist and somebody offers you money," Gaiman explains. "It was great. Not only did I pay the rent, but that biography bought me an electric typewriter."

Today, he is one of the most acclaimed comics writers of his generation, most notably for his epic World Fantasy Award–winning *Sandman* series (1989–96, collected into various volumes), *The Books of Magic* (1989), and *Death: The High Cost of Living* (1993). He is also the author of the novels *Neverwhere* (1996), *Stardust* (1999), *American Gods* (2001), *Anansi Boys* (2005), *Interworld* (2007, with Michael Reaves), *Odd and the Frost Giants* (2008), and *The Graveyard Book* (2008).

"People would say—like with *Stardust*—'Well, it's great, but it's not *Sandman*,'" he reveals. "And I'd say, 'Well, *Sandman* took me seven years to write, it's two thousand pages long, over ten volumes, it's enormous. *Stardust* was barely sixty thousand words. Why are you comparing these two?'"

Gaiman's other books include *Don't Panic: The Official Hitchhiker's Guide to the Galaxy Companion* (1988), *Ghastly Beyond Belief* (1984, with Kim Newman), *Now We Are Sick* (1991, with Stephen Jones), *The Sandman Book of Dreams* (1996, with Edward E. Kramer), *The Dangerous Alphabet* (2008, with Gris Grimly), and numerous graphic novel collaborations, most notably with artist Dave McKean. *Angels & Visitations: A Miscellany* (1993) is a best-selling collection of his short fiction that won the International Horror Guild Award. It was followed by *Smoke and Mirrors* (1998), *Adventures in the Dream Trade* (2002), *Fragile Things* (2006), and *M Is for Magic* (2007).

He created the 1996 BBC miniseries *Neverwhere* (with comedian Lenny Henry) and scripted the English-language version of Hayao Miyazaki's acclaimed *Princess Mononoke* (1999), a fifth-season episode of TNT's *Babylon 5* ("Day of the Dead," 1998), and Robert Zemeckis's 3-D motion-capture epic *Beowulf* (2007, written with Roger Avary). Gaiman also wrote and directed *A Short Film About John Bolton*

The Gaiman family enjoy a musical evening at home in England during the 1960s.

in 2003, while Mathew Vaughn's *Stardust* (2007) was adapted from his novel of the same name.

In the early 1990s, Neil Gaiman was beginning to make a name for himself as a writer of comic books. He had also recently collaborated on a very successful humorous novel *Good Omens: The Nice and Accurate Prophecies of Agnes Nutter, Witch* (1990), with best-selling author Terry Pratchett.

"My daughter Holly was about four or five years old," he recalls, "and she used to come home from school and she'd see me sitting and writing. She would then clamber up onto my knee and dictate little stories to me.

"These were normally about small girls named Holly, whose mothers would invariably be kidnapped by evil witches who looked like their mothers. Then the evil witches would lock them in cupboards and other places.

"They were scary, nightmarish four-year-old girl stories. And I thought, 'Well, she obviously likes this sort of thing, and I like this sort of thing. Why don't I go out and find a book like this for her?'

"But I couldn't find anything even remotely like that. So, I thought, 'Okay then, I'll write one.' So I started writing this book."

Neil Gaiman with his eldest daughter, Holly.

"*Coraline* was a story that my dad read me bits and pieces of when I was a little girl," Holly Gaiman remembers, "a story that he started writing for me, that nobody else had ever heard or read. It's a lovely story, one that's both haunted and inspired me since I was a little girl."

After completing three or four chapters in his own time while working on *Sandman,* in 1991 Gaiman took the pages up to London book publisher Victor Gollancz to show to his editor on *Good Omens.*

"He was a very nice, very perceptive, very brilliant man named Richard Evans," recalls the author. "So Richard read it, and the next time I saw him he said, 'Let's talk about that book you gave me, *Coraline.*'"

An experienced editor, Evans was extremely impressed by the chapters he had read, and told the young author that it was probably the best thing he had ever written. However, there was just one problem. Did he realize that it was not publishable?

"I said, 'No,'" Gaiman reveals. "'Why is it not publishable?' And he said, 'Well, because you're writing a novel that is aimed both at children and at adults. Nobody can publish something that is for *both* kids and adults.' You have to remember that this was long before *Harry Potter.*

"He also pointed out that it was a horror novel for children, and you can't publish *things like that.* Back then, you could absolutely publish gritty novels about heroin addiction on housing estates, but you couldn't publish horror fiction for children. There wasn't even much fantasy.

"Richard was absolutely right and, at that time, it was the best advice he could have given me."

Despite his initial disappointment, Gaiman was undeterred and decided to continue writing the book during whatever spare time he had.

But by now, in 1992, the increasingly successful author had moved his family to America, where they lived in a big, dark Addams Family–style house, where he accumulated computers and cats.

"Then I ran out of the entire concept of my own time," he recalls.

With his career taking off in numerous directions, it was another five or six years before Gaiman found time to again return to his novel about Coraline. In the interim he had added only another thousand words to the manuscript.

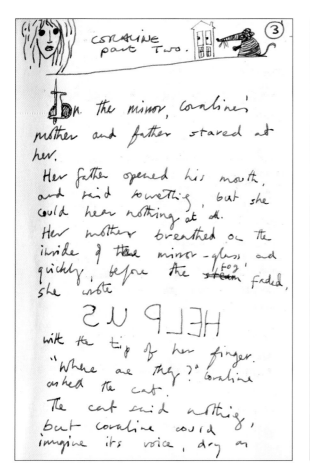

In the mirror, Coraline's mother and father stared at her.

Her father opened his mouth, and said something, but she could hear nothing at all.

Her mother breathed on the inside of the mirror-glass, and quickly, before the ~~steam~~ 'fog' faded, she wrote

HELP US

with the tip of her finger.

"Where are they?" Coraline asked the cat.

The cat said nothing, but Coraline could imagine its voice, dry as

could not name. It had not made her want to go in any further.

And this one...

If there was one thing of which Coraline was certain, it was that this one would be worse.

"I'm an explorer," she said out loud, but her words sounded muffled and dead in the misty air.

She knocked on the door. It swung open, and she walked in.

"We have eyes and we have nerveses we have ~~fingers~~ noses, we have toils, we have teeth. And you'll all get what you ~~suppose~~ deserveses when we come from underneath,"

"I looked around and suddenly thought, 'My daughter Holly, who I had started writing this for, is now getting too old for it.'"

Gaiman now had a second young daughter, Maddy, and he realized that if he did not finish the book soon, even she would be too old for it as well. "I needed a contract, as that was the only way it was ever going to get written. So I sent the manuscript—ten thousand words or whatever it was that existed—to my editor at Avon Books at that time, Jennifer Hershey."

As had happened with Richard Evans all those years earlier, Hershey loved what she had read. She still was not sure of which audience it was aimed at, but the difference this time was that she wanted to know what happened next.

"I said, 'Send me a contract and we will both find out,'" reveals Gaiman. "So she sent me the contract, and now I *had* to finish this book. I *really* had to finish it, except, the problem was, I still had no time to write it!"

With his youngest daughter growing up quickly and a contract now hanging over his head, Gaiman came up with a plan: "For the next two years, instead of reading in bed before I turned off the light, I would write."

Handwritten pages from Neil Gaiman's original manuscript for Coraline.

He began to keep a notebook beside his bed and before he went to sleep, each evening, instead of reading from a book, he would write fifty or a hundred words, maybe five or six lines.

"It was a very slow way of writing," he admits. "It's one page every six days, or something like that. But I was doing it every night, and the book would just keep creeping forward a little bit here and a little bit there until, eventually, I found myself approaching the end."

While on a Comic Book Legal Defense Fund cruise in 2000 with his son Michael, Gaiman started working on *Coraline* in earnest when he discovered that he had accidentally left his other notebook at home. Upon his return, he spent a week finishing off the novel.

Over the previous two years, the author had also been working on a major adult novel, *American Gods,* about the epic clash between the New Gods of modern technology and the Old Gods of ancient mythology.

"I got up one morning and I thought, if I don't finish something soon, I will go mad," says Gaiman. "So I took a week off from *American Gods,* wrote the final chapters of *Coraline* and sent it off to my various editors at what was now HarperCollins, saying, 'I know I'm late with *American Gods* but look here—I've finished a book. And they all said, 'That's very nice, now go and finish *American Gods.*'"

Coraline's new home, as envisioned by artist Dave McKean for the back cover of the original U.S. edition of Coraline. *"The house is actually a photo of the building in Forest Row where Neil used to live," explains McKean.*

Coraline is the story of a young girl named Coraline Jones.

Some adults think that her name is "Caroline," but that is because they are not listening very carefully.

"It's Coraline. Not Caroline. Coraline," said Coraline.

Coraline's mother and father love her very much, but they are distracted by the work that they do from home on their computers. They have just moved into a big Victorian house:

It was a very old house—it had an attic under the roof and a cellar under the ground and an overgrown garden with huge old trees in it.

Coraline's family didn't own all of the house, it was too big for that. Instead they owned part of it.

There were other people who lived in the old house.

Miss Spink and Miss Forcible lived in the flat below Coraline's, on the ground floor. They were both old and round, and they lived in their flat with a number of ageing highland terriers who had names like Hamish and Andrew and Jock. Once upon a time Miss Spink and Miss Forcible had been actresses . . . In the flat above Coraline's, under the roof, was a crazy old man with a big moustache. He told Coraline that he was training a mouse circus. He wouldn't let anyone see it.

Coraline likes exploring. One rainy afternoon, at her father's suggestion, she explores their new flat and, to pass the time, she counts everything blue (153), the windows (21), and the doors (14). Thirteen of the doors open and close.

The other, the big, carved, brown wooden door at the far corner of the drawing room, was locked.

Investigating further, Coraline discovers that the door doesn't go anywhere. It opens onto a brick wall. That is until the afternoon that Coraline unlocks the door and goes through it.

It opened onto a dark hallway. The bricks had gone as if they'd never been there. There was a cold, musty smell coming through the open doorway: it smelled like something very old and very slow.

She discovers that the corridor leads to another flat in another house that is just like her own.

Except it is different. . .

ABOVE LEFT

Dave McKean's preliminary sketch of Coraline meeting Miss Spink and Miss Forcible for the original U.S. edition of **Coraline.**

ABOVE RIGHT

Dave McKean's preliminary sketch of Mr. Bobo for the original U.S. edition of **Coraline.**

OPPOSITE TOP

Dave McKean's preliminary sketch of Coraline opening the mysterious door.

OPPOSITE BOTTOM

Dave McKean's finished artwork for the same scene, used in the U.S. edition of **Coraline.**

Elements of the house in *Coraline* are inspired by two real homes where Neil Gaiman once lived. Although the actual layout of the flat that Coraline and her family move into was based on Gaiman's apartment in the East Sussex village of Nutley, where he started writing the book, the door leading to the bricked-up hallway actually existed in the house in East Grinstead where the author lived between the ages of six and eleven years old.

"My parents bought a house that was half of a larger old manor house," he recalls. "It had been divided into two, and we lived in what would have been the servants' quarters, except for one really impressive oak-paneled living room that had two doors. One door went in and out. The other door, at the end of the room, opened onto a brick wall. But I was convinced that it wouldn't always open onto a brick wall, and as a small boy I used to try sneaking up on it whenever I'd go into that room.

"I'd lean against it, as if I was doing something else. Then I'd open it quickly and look. And it would always be a brick wall. But I was convinced that if only I approached it properly, if I sneaked up on it, one day there would be a corridor behind it.

"As a child, I had a dream where I opened the door and there *was* a tunnel and I went down it. In the book, Coraline finds a door that is bricked up. And one day she goes through that door, and there *is* a corridor. On the other side of the door she finds herself in a room in a flat that is a lot like the one that she has just left."

At first, the other flat appears to be wonderful. The food there is better. The toy box is crammed with wind-up angels that fly around the room, books where the pictures move in a marvelous manner, miniature dinosaur skulls that chatter their teeth...

But there is also the Other Mother.

> She looked a little like Coraline's mother. Only...
> Only her skin was white as paper.
> Only she was taller and thinner.
> Only her fingers were too long, and they never stopped moving, and her dark red fingernails were curved and sharp.

And, perhaps most disconcerting of all, she has big black buttons for eyes. So does the Other Father, and they want Coraline to be *their* little girl and stay with them forever. That is, once they have *changed* her...

"The buttons idea seemed cool and scary," explains Gaiman.

"There are some moments where you really wish you could just go back in time and talk to yourself. You could go back and say, 'Don't do that. Don't go out with him. Don't eat that. Don't listen to them,' whatever.

"I wish I could go back and just sit myself down and say, 'You're going to start writing this book called *Coraline,* and it will have an evil Other Mother in it who will have big black buttons for eyes. And when you get the idea, would you mind just remembering for yourself where the idea came from, what prompted it, and how you got it, because in a decade you will be asked this in interviews probably once every week.' And now, with the movie, I know that I am going to be asked it even more...

*D*ave McKean's preliminary sketch of Coraline's button-eyed Other Mother for the U.S. edition of **Coraline.**

"The only place I've thought about where there was any inspiration was in a story published in 1882, by a lady named Lucy Clifford, who wrote these really, really, disturbing stories for children.

"She wrote one story called 'The New Mother,' about these children who were basically told by their mother that if they are naughty then she will have to leave them, and their new mother will come.

"But they *are* naughty, and when they get home their mother is gone. Then they hear this clattering noise, and they look down the street and coming toward them from a long distance away they can see the flames glittering off the glass eyes of their new mother, and they can hear the *swish, swish, swish* of her wooden tail.

"So I think maybe that went somewhere into the mixture.

"There is also a tradition, which I think goes back to the Romans, of putting coins on the eyes of the dead. The idea that the eyes are the windows to the soul. With buttons you somehow lose all the things that make you human. It is the metaphor that allows for a hundred interpretations, or a thousand interpretations, and they are all correct."

The Other Mother and Other Father tell Coraline that she can stay with them as one big happy family forever and always, but only if she replaces her own eyes with two black buttons.

When Coraline refuses, she discovers that the Other Mother has trapped her real parents in the Other World. In an attempt to teach Coraline a lesson in manners, the Other Mother locks her in the darkness behind a mirror.

There she encounters three ghost children, lost hearts and souls imprisoned and forgotten long ago by the Other Mother in that dark and empty place.

> "She will take your life and all you are and all you carest for, and she will leave you with nothing but mist and fog. She'll take your joy. And one day you'll awake and your heart and your soul will have gone. A husk you'll be, a wisp you'll be, and a thing no more than a dream on waking, or a memory of something forgotten."

Coraline is their only hope of rescue. But to save the dead children, her kidnapped parents, and herself, she will have to use all her wits to win a hide-and-go-seek game with the Other Mother. And if she loses, then Coraline will have to stay in the Other World forever. . .

"I wanted to write about bravery," explains Neil Gaiman. "I wanted to write something that was about *being* brave.

"As a child I always thought that being brave meant not being scared. It wasn't until I was in my thirties that I figured out not being scared isn't brave. It's just not being scared. Being brave is being absolutely scared and doing what you *have* to do—despite fear, despite obstacles, despite anything. And I decided that I wanted to write a book that was about that.

"I also wanted to write a book about love. I wanted to write a book that said sometimes the people who love you may not pay you all the attention that you need. Sometimes the people who do pay you attention may not love you, or may not love you in healthy and good ways. I wanted to write a book that said *yes, there are monsters*.

"A good fairy tale should always have a monster or a dragon, but what is important about monsters is not that they exist but that they can be defeated.

"For me, that was what *Coraline* was all about. People say to me, 'You're putting ideas into children's heads.' But kids have these ideas anyway. Kids know that there are monsters under the bed. They know there are things in the shadows. Telling them that they are not there doesn't actually make things any better. But telling them that a dragon can be defeated, then that's important.

"One of the things that surprised me most about writing *Coraline* is that it was written over a period of ten years," says Neil Gaiman. "Yet from the very beginning, I knew the voice I wanted the book to have. Page one of *Coraline* has never changed since I wrote it.

"I knew that I wanted this very clean, classic English children's story kind of style all the way through. The writing is very, very flat. There's nothing colorful in the writing of *Coraline,* nothing clever. So the voice of the book is consistent throughout.

"I always knew what was going to happen except, of course, that when I started it I thought it was going to be around three thousand words, not thirty thousand.

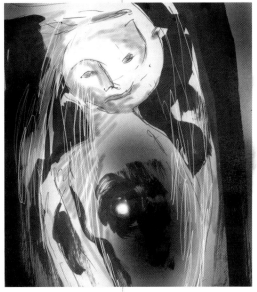

TOP

*D*ave McKean's preliminary sketch of Coraline's parents trapped in the snow globe. This illustration was not used in the finished book.

ABOVE

*D*ave McKean's preliminary sketch of the ghostly children. This was significantly revised for the finished book.

"For a long time *Coraline* felt to me like walking toward the horizon and the horizon was receding. I'd think I was almost done, and then I'd write a bit more, and then a bit more. I had known about the Other Mother's right hand all the way back on page one, and now it was ten years later and I had eventually reached the point where the Other Mother's hand was preparing for its final spring. And I thought, 'Yes . . . this is my book.'"

Having started the book a decade earlier for his daughter Holly, the author now needed another audience to try it out on.

"The joy of writing any book is that different people take different things away from it," explains Gaiman. "The first person I tried *Coraline* out on when I finished it was my daughter

Maddy. She was six going on seven at the time, and I said, 'Okay, I'm going to read you a book.'"

Maddy Gaiman recalls that she would listen to her father reading a chapter each night before she fell asleep: "Then he would reread me the whole chapter again, and I would just love it even more the second time. I remember when he finished it and I really liked it, and he was happy that I liked it."

"So we read it together over four or five nights," her father reveals, "and if she had been scared or troubled by it, if it really had disturbed her, then I probably would have just put it away. However, she loved it and wasn't noticeably scared or troubled by it at all."

"I think the book *Coraline* is one of the best children's books I have ever read," says Maddy Gaiman. "Not just because I think the author is great—because, of course, I do—but it is a story that really draws you in and keeps you there.

"You always want to know what's going to happen next. You really get attached to Coraline, rooting and hoping that she will come out on top. It's pretty much amazing."

Faced with that enthusiasm from his own daughter, the author sent the manuscript off to his literary agent, Merrilee Heifetz, in New York City.

"I said, 'Here you go, finish the book.' She phoned me back the following day and said, 'Are you seriously proposing that we publish this as a children's book?' And I replied, 'Well, yeah.' And she said, 'But it disturbed me.' And I said, 'And your point is?' She said, 'Well, you can't let children read this.' And I said, 'Well, you have two daughters, one is six and one is eight. Read it to them this week, and then call me back.'

"So she went away, read it to her children, Morgan and Emily, and phoned me back about five days later saying, 'They loved it. They weren't scared. It was just an adventure for them.' And I said, 'Yes, that seems to be how it's working.' So Merrilee sent it over to HarperCollins."

Around this time, the publishing industry on both sides of the Atlantic was going through a major transition. Nobody had foreseen the effect that the phenomenal success of J. K. Rowling's *Harry Potter* series would have on the way children's books would be published and marketed.

"*Coraline* was originally bought by a colleague of mine, Jennifer Hershey, at Avon Books, who edited all of Neil's work at the time," explains Elise Howard, now SVP, associate publisher, fiction, at HarperCollins Children's Books.

"I didn't work directly on the book then, but Jennifer would bring me chunks of it to read as Neil turned them in, and all my comments were along the lines of, 'Wow. This is really wonderful. More, please.'

"Neil is one of the most natural, intuitive writers that I've ever worked with—

*M*addy Gaiman
and a furry friend.

except that a closer reading of his work perhaps reveals just what a great reader he is, too, and how much he appreciates and acknowledges the work of other great writers—and his work is the kind that's a joy not just to read, but to reread."

"I was very, very fortunate in 2002," admits Gaiman. "Despite the fact that I had been writing this book for ten years, the publishing landscape had changed. The *Harry Potter* books had started coming out. Lemony Snicket and Philip Pullman were being published. And suddenly, the idea of a world in which you could publish a book that was for kids that adults would also read and enjoy— the idea of publishing something that was essentially a horror novel for children—was no longer a bizarre, ridiculous, or unlikely thing."

"When the Avon imprints became part of HarperCollins," Elise Howard reveals, "*Coraline* moved to the children's division, where I worked. Those of us at Harper knew what a great book *Coraline* was but, at the time, the market was not entirely friendly to the notion of a children's book by a writer of works primarily for adults. Such books often were considered minor, or somehow indulgent.

"Luckily, two major constituencies harbored no such prejudices. Librarians, who readily love and recognize great fiction of all sorts and cross boundaries easily, immediately embraced *Coraline*. Neil's established readership, hungry for whatever new idea sprung from the head of their author, saw that a book for children was just the latest new thing that Neil was trying and mastering."

Because *Coraline* would be marketed ostensibly as a book for children and young adults, HarperCollins decided that it should be illustrated. But when it came to choosing an artist, the candidate was not quite as obvious as it first appeared.

"My original choice for an illustrator for *Coraline* was Edward Gorey," reveals Neil Gaiman, "because I had always loved his work, and I thought that he would be the perfect choice of artist. Unfortunately, he died the day I finished writing the book.

"I had sent *Coraline* to Dave McKean for him to try out on his daughter, but I hadn't planned to ask him to illustrate it as I didn't actually think that it was his kind of thing."

Born in 1963 in Maidenhead, Berkshire, British illustrator Dave McKean first met Neil Gaiman following a trip to New York in 1986, when he failed to find work as a comic book artist. Teaming up, the pair collaborated on the ground-breaking graphic novel about childhood experiences, *Violent Cases* (1987).

The following year, they again worked together as artist and writer, respectively, on the prestige miniseries *Black Orchid,* for DC/Vertigo Comics. Starting in 1989, McKean began illustrating the unconventional covers to Gaiman's *Sandman* series at DC/Vertigo.

Since then, McKean and Gaiman have collaborated on various graphic novels and children's books, including *Signal to Noise* (1992), *The Tragical Comedy or Comical Tragedy of Mr. Punch* (1995), *The Day I Swapped My Dad for Two Goldfish* (1998), and *The Wolves in the Walls* (2003).

"I knew that Neil was writing *Coraline* for a couple of years before I read anything," recalls Dave McKean. "He would tell me bits and pieces about it as we waited for planes, or in restaurants.

"I think all Neil's best books and stories have had time to gestate in this manner, collecting in pieces on his laptop, before reaching a critical mass when the final book has to be written.

"He sent me the book via e-mail, and I read it to my daughter Yolanda. It's always interesting reading a book like this to children—their reactions are not predictable, and can definitely affect the way the illustrations would work with the text, what they would show, and what they would keep hidden."

However, at this point, the publisher was not all that keen on the idea of McKean illustrating the book, as they associated him with Gaiman's more mature graphic novels and comics.

*D*ave McKean's original cover design for the U.S. edition of **Coraline**. "I got cold feet about it and redid it," reveals the artist. It was eventually used as a frontispiece for the special edition from Subterranean Press.

Then the artist did an ink-and-wash illustration of Mister Bobo's mouse circus orchestra for a birthday card invitation for his daughter, which he also e-mailed to Gaiman. The author forwarded it to HarperCollins and McKean found himself not only hired to illustrate the book, but able to bring his personal vision to the artwork.

"Neil was happy to let me go my own way," the artist explains. "If I had any questions, especially about how Neil imagined the characters, then I asked. But generally, the set of illustrations grew easily out of the scenes in each chapter. The house I used was the one in which Neil used to own a flat, back when I first got to know him."

Having completed the sixteen, mostly full-page illustrations for the book in a week, McKean then turned his attention to the dust-jacket painting. Having initially produced an image that he wasn't wholly satisfied with, five days later the artist delivered the painting of Coraline holding a candle, with

ABOVE

Old friends Neil Gaiman and Dave McKean (seated).

RIGHT

Dave McKean's original ink-and-wash illustration of Mister Bobo's mouse circus orchestra for his daughter's birthday card invitation.

OPPOSITE

Dave McKean's cover painting for the original U.S. edition of **Coraline.**

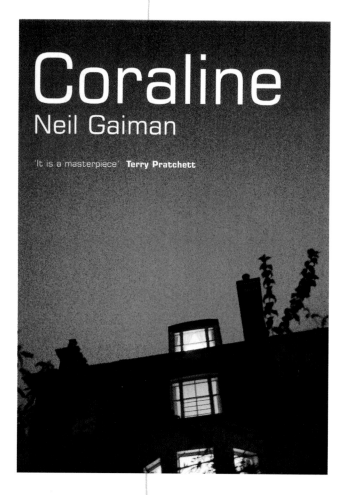

Coraline
Neil Gaiman

'It is a masterpiece' **Terry Pratchett**

The first British edition of Coraline.

instructions for a delicate spot-varnish effect to serve as a background.

"I designed the image," he reveals, "and requested the varnish plate be used to print a separate line art piece of the hands and mice. Depending on the angle of the book, the varnish disappears, or reflects the light to become very clear."

When the book was first published in Britain later the same year, it didn't include the interior art and also replaced McKean's atmospheric cover painting with a photograph of the exterior of a house at twilight.

As it turned out, when Bloomsbury reissued the book in a trade paperback edition the following year, it finally included the artist's work.

Not only did Bloomsbury's new edition reinstate most of McKean's artwork, but it also boasted a new cover painting of Coraline and the enigmatic black cat that helps her escape from the Other Mother.

Gaiman also scripted Dave McKean's debut as a feature film director, *MirrorMask,* which premiered at the Sundance Film Festival in January 2005. Combining live-action with digital animation, the film was a children's fantasy about a teenage girl who found herself in a bizarre fantasy world where the balance between Light and Darkness had been broken. The original story, a collaboration between the two old friends, shares a number of thematic similarities with *Coraline.*

"Of course it is similar to *Coraline,*" McKean agrees. "It is the same story as Alice, or the Wizard of Oz, or Narnia, or any number of fantasy stories. It is a dream, where the dreamer passes through a portal into a world that articulates their fears and anxieties in fantastical and metaphorical scenes.

"The success or failure of these stories depends on the imaginative success of these sequences, and how well the layers of fantasy, or dream, connect with a real-world situation.

"In *MirrorMask* we tried to create a crucial crossroads—a girl at a particular age, caught between childhood and young adulthood, and a situation that is pushing her to grow up and accept adult responsibilities before she is really ready. *Coraline* is much more about an important, and slightly younger, age, when a child's biggest fear

is being left alone. When the protagonist starts to feel that her parents have this other, alien and strange, life. An adult life that has context and emotional currents outside the safe world of 'mum and dad.'"

Dave McKean is also eager to point out that the book is more than just a good children's read: "Most of Neil's work takes established story shapes and plays with the reader's expectations of these shapes," he explains. "I thought *Coraline* was a neat metaphor for a child's slipping perception of their parents—from safe, sexless parents into complex, difficult, flawed people.

"This sounds like I think that the Other Mother is closer to an actual person than the real mother on the safe side of the door. And I think that's probably true."

McKean reveals: "It's the only working relationship I'm ever going to have in my life where I grow with my creative partner into a mature, clear-sighted collaborative

Dave McKean's wraparound cover painting for the British trade paperback edition of Coraline.

team. It's wonderful working with other people, and learning from them. But the feeling of continuity, and an ongoing conversation with Neil is irreplaceable.

"It's an unusual partnership, in that we are very different people, with very different tastes. But it is this friction, and basic trust, that has kept the friendship grounded and oiled."

"*Coraline* was just something that the publishers were very, very happy to take a chance with," says Gaiman. "2002 was the height of *Harry Potter* mania, but it was also the first year that J. K. Rowling had skipped a summer publication because she had missed her deadline.

"So suddenly, all of these column inches that had been reserved to write about the new *Harry Potter* book were now going spare. Through luck, more than anything else, we got this incredible amount of media attention that you would never normally get for a children's book.

"So the book came out and went straight onto the *New York Times* bestseller list."

As Elise Howard, the book's editor at HarperCollins, recalls: "Phillip Pullman, an author whose own books were loved by young and adult readers, praised the book and suggested that a standing ovation was in order. And then *USA Today* compared it to *The Chronicles of Narnia,* and a modern classic was born."

The influential review by Pullman, controversial author of the "His Dark Materials" trilogy of secular fantasy novels (*The Golden Compass, The Subtle Knife,* and *The*

Amber Spyglass), appeared under the title "The Other Mother" in the August 31, 2002, issue of the British newspaper *Guardian*. Pullman concluded his critique:

> There is much more. There is the creepy atmosphere of the other flat—the scariest apartment since the one in David Lynch's film *Lost Highway*; there is the tender and beautifully judged ending; and above all, there is Coraline herself, brave and frightened, self-reliant and doubtful, and finally triumphant. Ladies and gentlemen, boys and girls, rise to your feet and applaud: Coraline *is* the real thing.

Soon praise was coming from other esteemed children's authors on both sides of the Atlantic.

"This book tells a fascinating and disturbing story that frightened me nearly to death," admitted *A Series of Unfortunate Events* author, Lemony Snicket (Daniel Handler). "Unless you want to find yourself hiding under your bed, with your thumb in your mouth, trembling with fear and making terrible noises, I suggest that you step very slowly away from this book and go find another source of amusement, such as investigating an unsolved crime or making a small animal out of yarn."

"Discworld" series author, Terry Pratchett, agreed: "This book will send a shiver down your spine, out through your shoes, and into a taxi to the airport. It has the delicate horror of the finest fairy tales, and it is a masterpiece. And you will never think about buttons in quite the same way again."

"It is the most splendidly original, weird, and frightening book I have read," revealed Diana Wynne Jones, the writer of such children's classics as *Charmed Life* and *Howl's Moving Castle,* "and yet full of things children will love."

In America, *Coraline* quickly sold fifty thousand copies, mostly to adults who were already familiar with Neil Gaiman's byline.

"And then the magic started," explains the author. "Some of those adults started giving it to their children to read, and some of those adults were schoolteachers. Suddenly, because it is written in a very plain vocabulary and has an interesting story, they had a book that they could use for reluctant readers.

"Now it gets taught as a set text in a lot of schools, mostly due

ABOVE

Dave McKean's preliminary sketch of Coraline and her mother and father for the original U.S. edition of Coraline.

BELOW

Dave McKean's preliminary sketch of Coraline and the Cat, which became the frontispiece of the original U.S. edition of Coraline.

Dave McKean's preliminary sketch of the Cat attacking the Other Mother for the original U.S. edition of Coraline.

to the remarkable collection of awards it has received, and I get letters from children aged six and upward."

In fact, in an article in the Education supplement of the *Guardian* newspaper for January 3, 2006, Heather McLean specifically cited *Coraline* as one of the books being taught to special-needs and gifted children to aid in accelerated learning:

> To introduce Neil Gaiman's frightening fantasy, *Coraline,* on day one, [teacher Charlotte] Raby put a picture of a spooky house on PowerPoint and asked her students to list twenty words describing it. On day two she added eerie music to the picture and they thought of more words. Day three entailed happy music, which changed the children's perception of the house and made them start talking about the concept of genre. By the end of the week, the students were familiar with the picture of the house and the ideas of mood and atmosphere.

The article went on to explain that in the following week the teacher added other pictures and sounds to the presentation in a lesson that introduced the book's characters through pictures associated with them. These images included buttons and cats.

"They tend to get quite excited about it all," said Charlotte Raby, a teacher for gifted and talented children at St. Marks primary school in Brighton, who added that this approach to learning allowed her to "find out what they know and means the kids who normally find it hard to express themselves in class can show me what they can do."

Not surprisingly, Neil Gaiman has always been an advocate of literacy programs for young people. His advice to any would-be authors just starting out is very simple: "Write," he says. "Write, write, write, and read. Read, read, read everything you can. Read the stuff you know that you like, and that you love. Read all of that, and read anything else.

"Then write, and make sure that you finish things. Because it's very easy to start things and it's very, very hard to get to the end.

"Don't be a writer if you don't love it. It's a really hard thing to do. It's just you and a blank screen, and you're making stuff up. It's a very odd, very strange profession. There are much easier ways to make money and earn a living.

"But if you do have to do it, and if you're good at it, and if you enjoy it, then I can't think of anything better. There's certainly nothing else I'd want to do."

Since it was first published in 2002, *Coraline* has become a literary phenomenon that continues to delight readers of different ages all over the world. In the United States alone there are three different paperback editions in print, and combined sales have exceeded 300,000 copies. Worldwide, the novel has sold more than a million copies.

"The oddest thing about *Coraline* for me is that, of all of my books—and I've been translated into many languages—*Coraline* has been translated into the most languages," reveals Gaiman.

"It's in Icelandic, it's in Chinese, it's in Japanese, it's in Indonesian, it's in Korean, it's in every Scandinavian language, all the Eastern European countries. It's this book that's been around."

Indeed, *Coraline* has been translated into more than thirty different languages, and the book has appeared on numerous bestseller lists, including four weeks on the *New York Times* children's chart, as well as prominent sales lists in France, Italy, and the United Kingdom.

Because Gaiman's usual British publisher did not have a children's imprint, *Coraline* was submitted to a number of different U.K. publishers. Although almost every one responded enthusiastically, maintaining that they were big fans of Gaiman's previous work and describing the book as the next *Harry Potter,* only one imprint replied saying that they loved the book but

BELOW, LEFT TO RIGHT

Covers for the Korean, Japanese, and German editions of **Coraline.**

*D*ave McKean's
cover design for the
Subterranean Press
special edition of
Coraline.

had never heard of the author. They also just happened to already be the publishers of the *Harry Potter* series.

"I was sent *Coraline* by Neil's U.K. agent Dorie Simmonds," recalls Sarah Odedina, head of children's publishing at British imprint Bloomsbury, "and on reading it I realized that this author had a very special and unique voice—both gentle and coaching, and yet also deeply chilling! I loved it.

"I did not know Neil's work, so came to the novel without any knowledge of his already stellar standing in the world of fantasy and graphic novels. I think that this was a bonus for Neil in our publication plans, as we promoted him as a 'new author' to Bloomsbury, and I think got him some extra attention because of it."

"I thought to myself, it's not going to be the new *Harry Potter*," explains Gaiman, "because *Harry Potter* is a one-off phenomenon. The last thing I wanted was for my book to be included in a new line aimed at children and adults that only lasted two years. I would get a huge advance and everybody would be disappointed. On the other hand, Bloomsbury liked the story, they had nothing to prove, and they already had *Harry Potter* anyway."

Dave McKean's back cover design for the Subterranean Press special edition of **Coraline.**

"Neil has always struck me as a writer with a great deal of respect for his readers," adds Odedina, "as well as for the business of writing and publishing. I think he is an intelligent writer, whose books bear many readings, and each subsequent reading reveals further delicacies and delights—this is particularly true, for me, of his latest novel, *The Graveyard Book*.

"I also admire the fact that Neil works hard on his books, and works and reworks until he has the most polished, fluent, and delightful prose possible. Some authors rely on their editors for this level of attention, but Neil's dedication to writing a great book means he is also dedicated to do the work needed to take the book to that level."

When *Coraline* was eventually finished, Gaiman's older daughter, Holly, had initially refused to look at it, even though the story was originally started for her a

decade earlier. Now aged around sixteen, she finally agreed to read an advance proof copy that her father gave her at a science fiction convention in Texas.

"She went off and spent the next couple of days reading it," he recalls. "At the end of the convention she said, 'Well, I finished *Coraline*.' So I asked her, somewhat nervously, 'Were you too old for it?' And she looked at me with this expression of infinite pity and she replied, 'Dad, you're never too old for *Coraline*.'

"I was *so* relieved!"

Although the book is recommended for children aged eight and older, during the years since it was first published, it has developed a readership that now encompasses all ages.

"It is a different reading experience for adults," explains Neil Gaiman, "because, at the end of the day, children reading *Coraline* are reading about somebody much like them-selves, who is going up against something big and scary.

"For them, it's an adventure. They know from the word go that Coraline is going to be just fine. They know that she is going to go up against scary things, but no kid who has ever read it has actually worried that I would do anything horrible to her during the course of the book.

*D*ave McKean's finished illustration of Coraline and the Cat, which was used as the frontispiece for the original U.S. edition of **Coraline.**

"Adults, on the other hand, are reading about a child in danger, and that stirs up all sorts of emotions. We want to protect our kids.

"So when children are reading *Coraline*, and she's about to go through that door, they're going, 'Yes, go through the door, go through!' And all the adults are thinking, 'Don't do that. Don't go through the door!'

"The reactions to it are very different."

The fact that *Coraline* appeals to such a wide and diverse readership is reflected in the numerous awards and recommendations that the book has garnered from all areas of the literary establishment since it was first published in 2002.

In genre publishing it has not only been awarded the Horror Writers Association

Bram Stoker Award for Best Work for Young Readers, but it also won the prestigious Hugo and Nebula Awards presented by the science fiction community.

Other accolades bestowed upon the novel include a coveted American Library Association's Best Book for Young Adults, an ALA Notable Children's Book Award, a *Guardian* Unlimited Best of 2002 Award, a *School Library Journal* Best Book Award, a *Publishers Weekly* Best Book Award, a *Child* Magazine Best Book of the Year Award, a *Book* Magazine Best Book Award, a Bulletin of the Center for Children's Books Blue Ribbon Award, an inclusion in New York Public Library's One Hundred Titles for Reading and Sharing, a New York Public Library Book for the Teen Age selection, an IRA/CBC Children's Choice Award, a BookSense 76 pick, an Amazon.com Editors' Choice Award, The GreenManReview.com 2002 Best Book for Younger Readers Award, and a Bookslut 2002 pick of the year.

The unabridged audiobook of *Coraline,* read by the author himself with original music by Stephin Merritt's The Gothic Archies, was voted a *Publishers Weekly* Best New Audio.

"So far as I can tell, it still traumatizes adults," reveals Neil Gaiman. "But the kids still read it as an adventure, and every week brings packages of letters from schools, because now it has become a set text in schools around the world.

"I get these children writing me letters, telling me what they think the Other Mother should do next, or what Coraline's next adventure should be. They want to know things in the book, and occasionally they point out errors. They are just wonderful. There are kids out there for whom *Coraline* is simply their favorite book. They read it over and over, and they write to me about it. I just feel baffled, and honored, and delighted by it all."

"When I was in sixth grade, all my friends would come and tell me that they had just read the book and that they really enjoyed it," recalls Maddy Gaiman. "I guess other schools across the country are reading it too, which I have to say I think is pretty cool, actually."

"*Coraline* was really something that was written for my family," says Gaiman. "It was written to entertain Holly and Maddy when they were young, but now children all over the world are being entertained by it.

"As an author, you can't ask for more than that."

2

The Movie

We are small but we are many
We are many we are small
We were here before you rose
We will be here when you fall.

Around the same time that Neil Gaiman started writing *Coraline*, he happened to see *The Nightmare Before Christmas* the week it was released in movie theaters.

"I loved *The Nightmare Before Christmas*," he recalls. "I also liked parts of *James and the Giant Peach*. There is stuff in there that I thought was just brilliant.

"Henry Selick was on my radar as an interesting talent and a remarkable creative force. I kept hearing about Henry from people. When I was working with Miramax, they would say, 'We haven't found the right thing for him, but we want to work with Henry Selick.' And then I'd talk to my agent, John Levin at CAA, and he would say, 'There's a guy called Henry Selick, and you guys would like each other.'

"So I kept hearing about Henry. When I finished writing *Coraline*, I gave the manuscript to John and I said, 'You should probably send it to Henry Selick.' So John sent the manuscript to Henry, and he loved it."

OPPOSITE

Coraline discovers a secret door.

Visionary director Henry Selick was born in New Jersey in 1952. An avid artist since the age of three, he was inspired to become an animator after seeing Lotte Reinger's revolutionary silhouette cartoon *The Adventures of Prince Achmed* (*Die Abenteuer des Prinzen Achmed,* 1926) and Ray Harryhausen's stop-motion monsters in *The 7th Voyage of Sinbad* (1958).

After studying art at Syracuse University and at Central St. Martin's College of Art and Design in London, Selick enrolled in an animation program at CalArts, where he made two Academy Award–nominated student films, *Phases* and *Tube Tales*.

He then joined Walt Disney Studios, working as an animation trainee or "in-betweener" on such films as *Pete's Dragon* (1977) and *The Small One* (1978), finally becoming a full-fledged animator on *The Fox and the Hound* (1981). Selick was mentored at Disney by veteran animator Eric Larsen, and it was during this period that he met and worked with such other young animators as Tim Burton, Brad Bird, Rick Heinrichs, John Musker, and others, who were all destined to go on to greater things.

Using a grant from the National Endowment for the Arts, Selick took eight months off to make the independent short film *Seepage* (1981), using stop-motion and watercolor animation. After spending several years freelancing in San Francisco, where he created animated commercials for such products as Pillsbury baked goods and Ritz crackers, he contributed sequences to John Korty and Charles Swenson's

Twice Upon a Time (1983), which utilized a cut-out animation technique known as Lumage.

Selick next went on to storyboard scenes for Disney's live-action *Return to Oz* (1985) and a 1986 film version of the ballet *The Nutcracker,* based on the designs of children's writer and illustrator Maurice Sendak.

However, it was a series of animated station identifications for MTV and an award-winning six-minute pilot, which he wrote and directed for the network, *Slow Bob in the Lower Dimensions* (1991), that brought him once again to the attention of former colleague Tim Burton, who asked him to direct *The Nightmare Before Christmas.*

Burton had initially dreamed up the concept while still working as an animator at Disney, as Selick explains: "Tim had come up with the basic idea, and he and Rick Heinrichs, who was a creative partner of his, had sculpted such characters as Jack and Zero and Sandy Claws back in the early 1980s.

"The idea was inspired by *How the Grinch Stole Christmas,* but with a very unique twist in that it's the clash of two holidays, and someone's stealing the holiday. It's just that wonderful combination, that collision, which gives it strength."

Coraline is appalled when the Other Mother and Other Father suggest sewing shiny black buttons into her eyes.

*Coraline delivers a
big bundle of mail
to Mr. Bobinsky.*

Unfortunately for the filmmakers, the early 1980s were not the right time to pitch a stop-motion feature to the studio, and Disney rejected the project.

"Then Tim left and went on to great success," recalls Selick. "I think they liked the project, and saw that Tim was very successful with *Batman*. So I believe they wanted him to come back to the studio and do big movies for them—big successful films like *Batman*—and this was a gift to him to get him to come back."

The Nightmare Before Christmas took more than three and a half years to complete, and has since become a cult favorite around the world (especially in Japan), spawning an annual Halloween rerelease in 3-D and a significant amount of merchandise that continues to be available to this day.

"We knew that there would be a certain group of people who would like it," says Selick, "but we had no idea that it would keep going. It just had this life beyond its first release, growing from a cult-size audience to a very large cult audience of people dressed up in the costumes, with tattoos and with songs inspired by it. We could never have foreseen this."

In 1993, Selick again teamed with producer Tim Burton and Walt Disney to direct *James and the Giant Peach*, a combination of stop-motion animation and live action based on the classic children's book by British writer Roald Dahl.

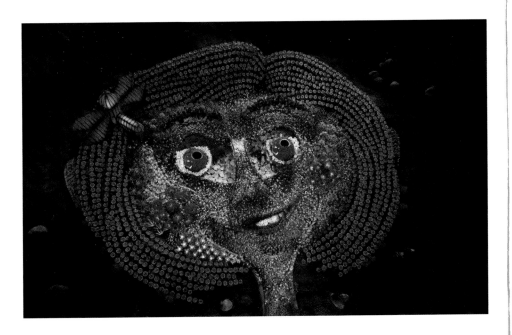

Coraline's portrait is created out of flowers in the Other Garden.

Selick's next film was *Monkeybone* (2001), another blend of live action and animation, loosely adapted from the graphic novel *Dark Town* by Kaja Blackley.

The filmmaker had been looking around for another project, when he was sent an advance manuscript of *Coraline* by Neil Gaiman's agent: "He thought of me as a possible director, someone to help turn it into a film. So I got the manuscript pages and I read them.

"When I first read *Coraline,* I was struck by this juxtaposition of worlds—the world we all live in, where we don't have a choice; and then a better version of all that, where the grass is always greener. That is very appealing. So I thought, right away, that this was something that everyone could relate to, and that was interesting to me.

"I also loved the fact that the grass-is-always-greener scenario turns out to be very scary indeed. Coraline doesn't have an easy job. What she has to go up against is incredibly dangerous and frightening, so that when she triumphs, it gives you the shivers. It really *means* something.

"Neil has said many times—and this may be one of the main attractions of the project for me—that you must face and defeat real evil for it to have meaning."

"So within a week Henry had read it," explains Gaiman, "and he came back and said that he wanted to do it." Former 20th Century Fox chairman and CEO Bill Mechanic bought the film rights to *Coraline*, and hired Selick to write the screenplay and direct.

"I love Neil Gaiman's stories," says Selick, "*Coraline* in particular. I think it is because not everything is new. He gives you something to hold on to—an archetype in terms

of characters, a storyline you might think you know, and then he reinvents it. In some ways Neil is a lot like Stephen King in setting fantasy in modern times, in our own lives. He splits open ordinary existence and finds magic there.

"Neil has got an incredible gift with language. He invites the reader in to participate. Neil's very charismatic, and so is his writing. It burns with a warm glow that is very attractive."

"So that's where it's all began," Gaiman adds. "Of course, since then it has taken more than seven years to get made. There have been a lot of ups and downs—who Henry was going to be making it with, and how he was going to make it—and eventually he went to LAIKA and they decided that they wanted to make it.

"It has taken a set of strange and wonderful coincidences to get us to where this movie was being made, but it all went back to that day with me sitting and watching *The Nightmare Before Christmas* and just thinking, 'This is lovely, this is wonderful.'"

"Henry wrote a script immediately," continues Gaiman. "However, the problem with the first script was that it was probably *too* faithful to the book. Then he wrote another script, and then another."

"*Coraline* is the story of a stubborn, skeptical, curious eleven-year-old girl," reveals Henry Selick, "who is forced to move, along with her parents, out of her comfortable life in Michigan to this huge, rambling old Victorian house outside Ashland, Oregon. Her mother and father love her, but they're too busy to give her the attention she needs.

"There's a rundown garden area with fish ponds. There's an old apple orchard. And vast fields surround the house. There are also worlds within the house itself.

"The house is divided up into multiple apartments, and Coraline is quite surprised when she gets there to learn this. That's another insult added to the injury of moving.

"Upstairs, a sad Russian giant lives in the attic. Sergei Alexander Bobinsky claims to be training a mouse circus and can't get Coraline's name right. Downstairs in the basement flat are these two eccentric old British actresses, Miss Spink and Miss Forcible. They live in an imaginary world with their three Scottie dogs—Hamish, Jock, and Angus. They are into the occult as a hobby, and like to corner people such as Coraline to tell them tales of when they were famous.

"There's also a really annoying neighborhood kid, Wybie Lovat, who is very territorial. His grandmother, in fact, owns the house, known as the 'Pink Palace,' that

Coraline and her parents have moved into. Wybie suggests that his grandma doesn't really like children living in the house, so he's surprised that Coraline's been allowed to live there.

"Coraline's life in Oregon looks pretty dreadful. Then one day, while aimlessly counting doors and windows in her new home, she discovers a small door hidden behind the wallpaper in the living room. She convinces her mother to find the key and open up that door, only to discover a brick wall.

"Well, Coraline is very curious, and also quite disappointed. However, in a dream that night, she's led to this door by glowing, jumping mice. And in her dreams, the bricks are gone. After going through the door, at the end of the passageway she finds an apartment just like her own—only nicer.

"She also discovers parents just like her own—but better. Her Other Mother and Other Father are funnier, warmer, more loving. They cook delicious food for her. They write songs for her, and want to play games with her. They even look better than her real parents—except her Other Parents have little black buttons for eyes, which should be a clue to Coraline that something is amiss. There's even a copy of the annoying Wybie, only in this world he's sweet and can't talk.

"Coraline soon learns that it is not a dream. When she first enters the Other World, it has a warmth, bright colors, a life to it. During subsequent visits, she discovers things like the garden—which is pretty much decrepit in the real world—is now a fantasy garden with living plants.

"Her Other Father is riding a mechanical praying-mantis tractor, planting seeds that immediately flower behind him. There are iridescent hummingbirds that light up each flower. There are snapping snapdragons that tickle her, and she's flown up into the air on the back of this flying tractor to see that the garden is a beautiful portrait of her face.

"Downstairs, in the real world, these old actresses, Miss Spink and Miss Forcible, live in a fairly cramped, uncomfortable place illuminated by candles. But in the Other World, their living space is transformed into a huge theater filled with hundreds of Scottie dogs in attendance, and they perform on stage there.

"So there are these amazing transformations. In the attic apartment, Mr. Bobinsky claims to be training a mouse circus. But in the Other World, he really does have a mouse circus. It's a miniature little tent with cotton-candy cannons and chicken popcorn poppers. Inside this little circus tent is a jumping mouse circus that performs and spells out Coraline's name.

"However, she also learns that this Other World is not quite as perfect as she first thought. When she tries to return home to her real parents, who love her very much, the Other Mother locks her in a closet-prison until she can learn some manners and be a '*loving* daughter.' She calls it 'love,' but we understand that it's something else.

"In the closet, Coraline meets the ghosts of three children who came before her. From them she learns what the Other Mother really is: a 'beldam'—a witch—who feeds on the lives of the children she lures to the Other World.

"With the help of the Other Wybie, Coraline manages to escape from the Other World, which has now turned creepy and dangerous. But once she's back home in her real apartment, she discovers that her real parents are missing—the Other Mother has trapped them in the Other World in order to lure Coraline back into her web."

Coraline pleads with her mother to find the key that will open the hidden door.

LEFT
*Coraline's Other
Parents welcome
her with a home-
cooked meal.*

ABOVE
*Coraline and
her Other Parents
enjoy breakfast
and dinner.*

RIGHT

*C*oraline is tickled by a gang of
naughty snapping snapdragons in the
Other Garden.

ABOVE

*T*he Other Father calls out to Coraline
from his Praying Mantis Tractor.

FOLLOWING PAGES

*M*r. Bobinsky's jumping mouse circus
spells out Coraline's name.

OPPOSITE

The Other Wybie gets
covered in cotton candy cones
fired out of cannons at the
miniature mouse circus.

ABOVE

Coraline refuses to apologize
to the Other Mother.

The Movie   47

OPPOSITE

*T*he Other Mother shoves Coraline
into the closet-prison and tells her
that she can't come out until she has
"Learned to be a loving daughter!"

ABOVE

*C*oraline meets the three ghost
children who are also trapped
in the closet.

TOP

The Other Wybie helps Coraline escape from the closet.

RIGHT

Coraline uses a phone to speed dial her missing parents.

OPPOSITE

Coraline sees in the hallway mirror that her parents have been taken by the Other Mother.

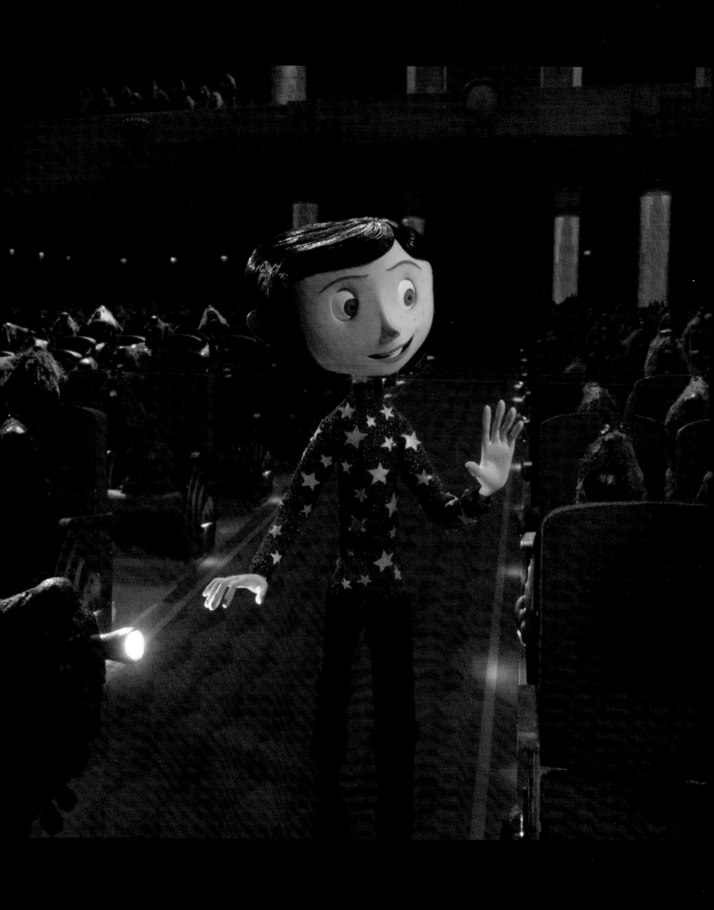

"There's an awful lot of Henry in the movie," reveals Neil Gaiman. "He hasn't taken the approach of, say, 'I'm going to make a movie out of Neil's novel and frame-for-frame it will be exactly what the book is.' He's played with it. He's turned it into *his* film."

"The screenplay is less creepy than the book," says Selick. "It's now more of a 'Hansel and Gretel' seduction into a place that appears to be colorful and wonderful, but turns out to be something more challenging. It is still as dark in moments, but also funnier and lighter in others. It has a little more balance."

"What's fun for me with the movie," Gaiman adds, "is I feel like Henry took that schematic that I gave him and then created this film. It's still *Coraline,* but as seen through Henry's world.

"I'm just terribly happy that Henry managed by sheer force of never giving up to get this film made. If there is one thing I've learned from the time that I've spent knocking around on the fringes of Hollywood while doing other things, it is how very, very hard it is to get a movie made.

"That Henry managed never to let this go, and to get it to the point where he actually called 'action' for the first time, just makes me so happy."

In September 2004, Bill Mechanic sold the film rights to Neil Gaiman's novel to Will Vinton Studios (later LAIKA) as a project for Henry Selick to direct. Bill Mechanic, founder and head of Pandemonium Films, would produce.

"Working with a director of Henry Selick's caliber is the perfect scenario

OPPOSITE
Coraline greets the Other Wybie before Miss Spink and Miss Forcible's show begins.

BELOW
Director Henry Selick behind the scenes on the Other Garden set.

for our project," explains former 20th Century Fox chairman and CEO Mechanic, whose previous credits as an independent producer include the J-horror remake *Dark Water* (2005) and Terrence Malick's *The New World* (2005). "We want to be partnered with visionary filmmakers in projects like *Coraline*, which take time-honored motifs—in this case a classic ghost story—and use modern techniques like animation to tell a compelling, unforgettable, and entertaining story."

"Coraline presents me with the perfect opportunity to take all I know about storytelling through animation," says Selick, "and bring those tools to bear on a story of a fascinating and spunky title character, who confronts some really scary stuff when

she walks through the doorway into a parallel universe where initially pleasant discoveries take on a much more sinister hue."

"Henry is an artist," enthuses Neil Gaiman, "and I think that's a really important thing. He has a vision, he has a sense of humor. He has a very specific idea of what he wants and he will go for it.

"He understands something that people often forget—that children love to be scared. Kids love to see cool stuff. I remember the joy for me of seeing *The Nightmare Before Christmas,* and just walking out of the theater afterward and thinking, 'Why aren't all movies like this?'

"He just seemed the obvious person who could take *Coraline* and make something special and strange with it. And, frankly, he had too much fun doing that."

Early in the production process, Selick and his producers talked about the use of distinct English accents in *Coraline,* as well as discussing where the film was to be set. Although Gaiman's original novel was implicitly based in the United Kingdom, Selick moved the action to America so that the film would appeal to a wider audience.

"He set it in Ashland, Oregon," Gaiman explains. "Henry was probably expecting me to fight about it, but I didn't. So far as I am concerned, the story is universal. I don't mind where it's set.

"I just wanted to make sure that Miss Spink and Miss Forcible were English, because there's a particular elderly, English, full-bosom spinsterhood that you don't really seem to run into quite so much elsewhere."

"We do have some English characters," Selick admits, "but it's just one of those things where it felt like the right idea."

RIGHT

Tadahiro's character design for Coraline and her Other Mother and Other Father.

BELOW

Tadahiro's concept design for Coraline being tucked into bed by her Other Mother and Other Father.

"My part in getting this movie made for many years consisted of me phoning Henry once every six or seven months and being encouraging," says Neil Gaiman. "I told him, 'You will get there. It will be okay. I'm keeping my fingers crossed for you, Henry. No, I'm not taking the rights back. Hang in there.'

"When it started to look like *Coraline* was finally happening, he would e-mail me his initial drawings."

"I was going for a classic storybook look," reveals Henry Selick, "but not in the way of, say, Disney films. I mean, I love movies like *Pinocchio* and *Bambi,* but I was actually going for a more graphic style. I found a famous artist, Tadahiro Uesugi, who is actually very much inspired by American illustrators of the late 1950s and early 1960s."

Born in 1966 in Miyazaki on Kyushu Island, Tadahiro is a world-renowned Japanese illustrator whose intuitive and elegant drawings have graced magazine covers, books, and various prestigious advertising campaigns in his native country, as well as in the United States and Europe.

When Selick decided that he wanted to take the character design in *Coraline* in a different direction from Dave McKean's distinctive artwork in the original book, he brought Tadahiro on board as the project's pre-production illustrator.

"I wanted to get a strong graphic look," explains the director, "compelling shapes that could exist in a 2-D space, so that when Coraline goes into the Other World—which we shot in 3-D—we could bring those graphic images to life. It would be surprising and inviting, and I don't actually think it's ever been done before."

"The style of the *Coraline* movie reminds me in some ways of the Japanese illustrations for the *Coraline* book," says Gaiman, "which has a different mood from the beautiful Dave McKean illustrations that we have in the American edition."

As a filmmaker himself, McKean is not too disappointed that Henry Selick's film adaptation does not utilize his style or design. "A book is a book, and a film is a film," insists the artist, "and they have very different demands weighing on them. My book drawings only have to work fleetingly in a moment, whereas Henry's character designs have to live and breathe on the screen for ninety minutes."

After working on the concept art in his native Japan for more than a year, Tadahiro briefly visited the LAIKA studios in Portland to observe firsthand how the production was progressing.

While at the Oregon facility, Tadahiro met with Canadian illustrator Michel Breton. Tadahiro taught the in-house designer how to work with his brushstrokes and palette of colors, so that the two of them could collaborate on designs, even though they were both based on different continents.

Once a draft of the script was completed that was approved by everybody, *Coraline* entered its preproduction stage in 2005 with the art direction and storyboarding processes. The task of visualizing every scene and character in the script was the responsibility of head story artist Chris Butler and his team of four storyboard illustrators.

"When you start getting into the script," explains Butler, who worked directly with Henry Selick, "you realize there are things that maybe don't work or could be improved upon. Or there are good things in it that, when you visualize them, give you new ideas.

ABOVE

Tadahiro's concept design for Coraline and the mouse circus.

BELOW

Tadahiro's concept design for Coraline in the Other Garden.

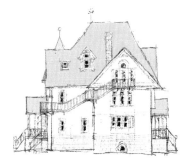

ABOVE

Tadahiro collaborated with Michel Breton on various concept designs. These are different views of the Pink Palace Apartments.

BELOW

Second assistant director Dan Pascall checks information on the big boards in the Production Alley at LAIKA studios.

"A lot of the time, the story department is actually bringing more to the story and creating new ideas, changing old ones, and reshaping the script. Because animation is so time-consuming and expensive, you need to know exactly what you're shooting before you start. It's not like live action—where you can use multiple cameras or do retakes. These things take so long, and the animators are moving one frame at a time, so you need to know *exactly* what shot you're getting before you actually do it.

"The benefit of the storyboards is that, instead of shooting directly from the script, we take the script and work out the entire movie in advance in picture form. Then we can take that material straight to the camera department.

"Doing storyboards is a lot like drawing comic book panels. However, whereas comic art is about getting an idea across dynamically and quickly, in a movie one small action might require multiple storyboard panels, because it's depicting complicated action or getting across a very important story point or a very important emotion. That might require something like twelve drawings. Of course, sometimes you don't need that many at all. It could be someone jumping from one side of the room to the other, and that's two drawings.

"How much detail you go into in the storyboard panels usually depends either on the director or on the complexity of the story."

To create the storyboards, Chris Butler and his team of artists used Wacom's Cintiq LCD flat-screen monitors. By using the interactive pen directly on the screen, the illustrators worked more quickly and intuitively.

The pixel-level pen features more than a thousand levels of pressure sensitivity on the pen-tip and eraser for precise image control, while the screens have adjustable stands that allow the artist to pivot or angle the display they are creating so as to achieve the optimal working angles.

"When I first came to LAIKA, I was a paper-and-pencil person," confesses the British-born Butler, whose previous credits include Walt Disney's *Tarzan II* (2005) and *Tim Burton's Corpse Bride* (2005). "I was probably the oldest storyboard artist on the crew to join at that point, as they had already been going for eight months.

"When I first came on board, everyone else was using Cintiqs and I was horrified. I demanded that they stock up on notepads and pencils. I tried to continue that way for about two weeks, and then someone forced me to have a go on the Cintiq. Within two days I was sold, and I never want to see paper ever again.

"The Cintiq is brilliant, because it means that the work is more contained. It allows you to do so much more in a much shorter time, and that does help."

Ean McNamara worked for more than a year on *Coraline,* first in the design department and then as an assistant storyboard artist/illustrator.

Production illustrator and designer Michel Breton works on a Cintiq to create the detailed environmental backgrounds for the world of Coraline.

"The great thing about stop-motion is that it's interdisciplinary," he explains. "You can do anything on a stop-motion film. You have the ability to make things with your hands, or you can make things on the computer—you can sculpt with light."

McNamara believes that, for the story artists, the advantages of using the Cintiq system are speed and the lack of generation loss. "If you're working by hand, you're going to end up scanning things into the computer and that is considered a generation. Just like if you copy a videotape over again and again, the quality will get worse and worse. In this case, your drawings don't get worse, but you end up just spending more time working to deliver an image than actually doing it."

The Cintiq's accurate brush control and selective application of effects and filters results in a digital on-screen experience that mirrors a traditional pen-on-paper feel, which was important when the storyboard artists had to create so many atmospheric images for *Coraline*.

"It's also amazing how much of a difference it has made when you are trying to get across a mood," reveals Chris Butler. "Much of this movie has a dark fairy-tale aspect to it, so we tried to make the drawings as atmospheric as possible, adding tone, because if it is just line drawings then it's not very scary.

"Being able to apply such varied amounts of tone onto just single panels really makes a difference when you cut it into the anamatic and watch it. That is essentially what we were doing—building the entire movie out of our storybook panels with sound, music, and dialogue, and then watching it to make sure that everything was working."

OPPOSITE
Coraline and the Cat watch the button-eyed doll burn in the fireplace.

LEFT
Behind the scenes, Henry Selick demonstrates his idea for a shot involving a reflective surface and a Coraline puppet.

Having had extensive experience himself as a storyboard artist—ever since he began making his own short films—Henry Selick is acutely aware of how crucial the process is for developing ideas and moving forward the preproduction process.

"In the 1980s," he recalls, "I was a story artist under Walter Murch—the brilliant film editor and sound designer—on a movie he directed called *Return to Oz*. Although it was a live-action film, Walter, as an editor, wanted to storyboard the whole film first. It was my job to take a written scene and then sketch out the best, most imaginative version of it that I could. Walter would come by to review my work, compliment me, and then tell me to come up with another way to do the scene.

"At first, it was as if I was a potter making the most beautiful ceramic cup I possibly could, only to have the boss nod appreciatively and then smash it on the ground and ask for another. Eventually, Walter would ask me to move on to another scene, and I learned to trust both him and this process of creation and destruction.

"In an animated feature film, you essentially make the film two times and backward. The first version of the film is made by sketching out the entire screenplay in storyboard drawings that, when played sequentially with dialogue and music (often temp in the early days of a production) give a sense of what the film will be.

"Over time, individual sequences are reconsidered, rewritten, reworked, and ultimately transformed into a very tight blueprint for shooting the second, or 'real' version of the film. No matter how good a script you start with, you will—if you have a clue as a director and your story team has talent—find a better way to do every scene than what was first written. You are essentially 'shooting coverage' and editing the film before you actually make the film—backward from live-action."

"What I like best about Henry is his sensibilities," continues Chris Butler. "He doesn't take the easy option story-wise. He doesn't want to follow the formula, and I for one would much rather work on an animated movie that pushes things in a slightly different way. A movie that tries to be a bit more bold, and maybe a bit more true.

"That's something that Henry was really serious about doing on *Coraline,* and I was with that absolutely 100 percent. He's incredibly demanding. He has a very strong vision."

"Story artists have to be great at drawing," explains Selick, "although it's less about beauty than clarity—they have to be strong visual storytellers who can get across a gag, or danger, or sweetness with a sketch or three. They should also be budding filmmakers themselves, who understand how their sequential drawings represent the actual film to come. On top of all this, they must accept that a good director is going to change or reject a lot of good storyboards in his search for what's best for the film."

"Animation is always going to be a collaborative process," agrees Butler. "That's what draws a lot of people to it, and what makes it so unique. But that has also meant that, on a lot of projects that I've worked on in the past, you have boardrooms full

of people all throwing their ideas into the pot. And what you end up with is no-one's vision.

"This movie is categorically Henry's vision, and having a really strong director like that you know you're going to have a very strong final film.

"I have to admit that there were a few instances where he came up with an idea and I thought, 'That's not going to work.' But I've drawn it anyway and then, three weeks down the line, you see it and it really works. That happened a few times, but I'm big enough to accept that."

Henry Selick is quick to praise his storyboard team on *Coraline*: "With the brilliant Chris Butler as head story artist working with the very talented Graham Annable and Vera Brosgol (along with a couple of other solid artists), this film had as good a story department as I've ever worked with."

With the script completed and storyboard designs underway by the end of 2006, the filmmakers at LAIKA next had to decide how best to create Coraline's two mirror worlds. Among the options discussed were computer animation (CG), stop-motion animation, or even a combination of the two.

"When Henry was first going to make the film at LAIKA," Neil Gaiman recalls, "it still wasn't definitely stop-motion. He talked about doing half of it as stop-motion and the other half computer animation. For a while they talked about making it CG before Coraline goes through the door, and then stop-motion, or even the other way around."

Initially, another alternative was also considered. "At that time the idea was that it was going to be a live-action movie," Gaiman reveals. "But somewhere in there, I think Henry became disillusioned with live action.

"I think he realized that what he loves is making movies. And what Henry is brilliant at is stop-motion. It is a gift. The truth is that I am really glad that he decided to make it in the way that he did."

"It's an *Alice in Wonderland* sort of story," says Selick. "I thought it was a perfect film for stop-motion animation."

In fact, the art of stop-motion animation has been around almost since the birth of cinema itself.

A highly detailed and meticulous process, it involves the frame-by-frame manipulation of a physical object to make it appear to move on its own. This is achieved by moving a jointed or malleable figure very slightly, exposing a photographic or digital frame, and then repeating the process twenty-four times to produce one second of film. When the many thousands of frames of a finished animation sequence are projected, the illusion is that the figure is animated in a fluid and continuous movement.

"It's a technique we used in *The Nightmare Before Christmas* and *James and the Giant Peach*," explains Selick. "We use armature puppets. You move them in tiny increments, twenty-four times per second, to create the illusion of motion.

"The miracle of stop-motion, and one of the reasons it's so magical for me, is what you see when you see a stop-motion animated character come to life, is an actual *performance* through the puppet by the animator. They start the first frame, and they have to move forward, trying to hit their marks like any live actor would. They try to say their lines at the right place. It's a real performance."

The very first example of cinematic stop-motion is usually credited to the 1898 short *The Humpty Dumpty Circus,* in which British émigrés Albert E. Smith and James Stuart Blackton used the pioneering technique to bring a toy circus of animals and acrobats to life.

Although such European animators as Lotte

RIGHT

*T*adahiro's early character designs for Coraline.

BELOW

*T*adahiro's designs were then re-created as three-dimensional maquettes.

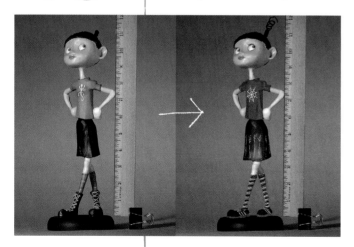

Reiniger, Ladyslaw Starewicz, and Alexander Ptushko were the first to use puppets and other objects to relate a coherent narrative, it was Californian Willis Harold O'Brien ("Obie" to his friends) who saw the commercial possibilities of the technique.

Around 1915, O'Brien began experimenting with filming a one-minute test reel featuring a miniature dinosaur and a caveman constructed from modeling clay over crude wooden skeletons. During the next decade, O'Brien expanded his techniques through a series of short films, including *Nippy's Nightmares* (1916), which was the first film to combine live actors with stop-motion characters.

After meeting nineteen-year-old Mexican sculptor Marcel Delgado, O'Brien was finally given the opportunity by First National Pictures to create the special effects for a $1 million adaptation of Sir Arthur Conan Doyle's adventure novel *The Lost World*, about the discovery of a plateau where dinosaurs still existed. The film took two years to complete, and after a ten-hour day, O'Brien's intricate and time-consuming work would be lucky to result in thirty-five feet of film (or thirty seconds screen time).

But O'Brien and his team persevered and, in February 1925, *The Lost World* opened at New York's Astor Theater to critical acclaim and went on to become a huge box-office hit.

Three years earlier, Conan Doyle had been a guest of Harry Houdini at a dinner for the American Society of Magicians held at the Hotel McAlpin in New York City. After being entertained by his hosts, at one A.M., the creator of Sherlock Holmes and a strong believer in spiritualism set up a movie projector and screen and then proceeded to astound his audience with moving pictures of dinosaurs and other prehistoric beasts that had been believed to have been extinct for millions of years. In fact, the footage had been created by O'Brien as a test for *The Lost World*.

Willis O'Brien moved to RKO Radio Pictures in 1929, and it was there that he and Delgado refined the latter's meticulous ball-and-socket metal armatures to create "The Eighth Wonder of the World"—the original *King Kong* (1933).

"The completed shots represented the ultimate in applied talents," O'Brien later recalled, "creating the ultimate picture."

King Kong was a massive hit around the world and, although O'Brien's career would never reach such a peak again, he did eventually receive a long-

The LAIKA team shot various characters from unique angles, such as this view of Mr. Bobinsky.

RIGHT AND BELOW

*Behind the scenes,
Coraline's mother
and father are
trapped in the
frosty snow globe.*

overdue Oscar for best special effects from the Academy of Motion Picture Arts and Sciences for his work on *Mighty Joe Young* (1949).

One of Willis H. O'Brien's apprentices on that film was twenty-eight-year-old Ray Harryhausen, who went on to improve upon his mentor's techniques (under the appellative "Dynamation") and inspire many generations of animators—including Henry Selick, who refers to Harryhausen as one of his "heroes"—by expertly combining his stop-motion aliens, prehistoric monsters, and mythological creatures with live-action elements in such films as *The Beast from 20,000 Fathoms* (1953), *20 Million Miles to Earth* (1957), *The 7th Voyage of Sinbad* (1958), and *Jason and the Argonauts* (1963).

Meanwhile, Hungarian animator George Pal (György Pál Marczincsák) had arrived in Hollywood in the early 1940s, where he produced a series of "Puppetoon" films for Paramount Pictures.

Unlike O'Brien and Harryhausen's "stop-motion" techniques, Pal's short films used "replacement" animation, which required up to nine thousand individually hand-carved wooden puppets or parts, each slightly different, to be filmed frame-by-frame to convey the illusion of movement.

Several "Puppetoon" films were nominated for Oscars, and Pal himself received an honorary Academy Award in 1944 for "the development of novel methods and techniques in the production of short subjects known as 'Puppetoons.'"

Pal later became a successful producer of fantasy and science fiction films, but continued to use puppet animation in such feature-length productions as *The Great Rupert* (1949), *Tom Thumb* (1958), and *The Wonderful World of the Brothers Grimm* (1963).

In the early 1960s, Arthur Rankin Jr. and Jules Bass cofounded Videocraft International. Using a stop-motion puppet process they dubbed "Animagic," Rankin/Bass produced such fondly remembered Christmas TV specials as *Rudolph the Red-Nosed Reindeer* (1964), *Frosty the Snowman* (1969), and *Santa Claus in Comin' to Town* (1970). Jules Bass also directed the feature films *The Daydreamer* (1966) and *Mad Monster Party?* (1967), utilizing the same process and both featuring the voice of Boris Karloff, among others.

For many years it looked as if the advances made in computer-generated imagery

Coraline holds the snow globe that will later become her parents' prison.

ABOVE

Behind the scenes, the Other World house is made to look very inviting.

OPPOSITE TOP

LAIKA chairman Philip H. Knight visits with director Henry Selick behind the scenes on Coraline.

OPPOSITE BOTTOM

Animator Chris Tichborne animates Coraline on an exterior Other World house set.

(CGI) would render the much more expensive and intricate stop-motion animation obsolete as a commercial filmmaking tool.

But then, in 1982, a young conceptual artist at Walt Disney was given $60,000 to create a six-minute stop-motion film based on his macabre poem. That individual was Tim Burton and, together with Disney animator Rick Heinrichs, he came up with *Vincent*. Shot in expressionist black-and-white, the experimental short was about a young boy who idolized actor Vincent Price and author Edgar Allan Poe, with the veteran horror-film star himself providing the narration.

A decade later, and with such box-office hits to his credit as *Beetle Juice* (1988), *Batman* (1989), and *Edward Scissorhands* (1990), Burton decided to put together a hand-picked team of artists and animators to create the ground-breaking stop-motion musical *Tim Burton's The Nightmare Before Christmas* (1993).

It was the first time that a fully animated project had been conceived on that scale, and although Burton acted as producer and came up with the original story, he turned to one-time fellow Disney employee Henry Selick to direct.

"It was a very, very hard project," recalls Selick, "but we knew it was going to be a pretty cool movie. What we did with *The Nightmare Before Christmas* was we really took it into a new arena of stop-motion in terms of camera moves, lighting, mood, and so forth."

In mid-2004, after creating the animated marine-life sequences for Wes Anderson's critically acclaimed *The Life Aquatic with Steve Zissou* (2004), Henry Selick joined the Oregon-based animation studio LAIKA as supervising director for feature-film development.

In 2003, entrepreneur and businessman Philip H. Knight invested in Vinton Studios. Originally founded by veteran animator Will Vinton, the studio had built a thirty-year legacy of excellence with "claymation" commercials and television projects such as the classic California Raisins and M&Ms campaigns, and the Emmy Award–winning UPN series *The PJs* (produced in conjunction with Imagine Entertainment and Eddie Murphy Productions).

Vinton lost control of the studio later that same year after failing to secure further investment, and Knight absorbed the company into a new venture, which in July 2005 was officially christened LAIKA, after the pioneering Soviet space dog that in 1957 became the first living mammal launched into orbit.

Today, with a staff of award-winning filmmakers, animators, and designers, LAIKA produces animation for films, commercials, music videos, and other media, using a wide range of techniques.

Phil Knight's son Travis is vice president of animation at the studio. He is also one of the lead animators on *Coraline*.

RIGHT

Miss Spink and Miss Forcible's basement apartment set.

BELOW

A behind-the-scenes view of the interior of the Other Mr. Bobinsky's mouse circus tent.

"LAIKA is a community of people who love animation," he explains, "and want to really do something interesting, unique, and innovative in the field. The company has its roots in stop-motion, and I think that informs a lot of our approaches to things. People who are involved in stop-motion are generally a peculiar breed. But that attitude, that feeling, tends to infiltrate the whole company.

"It's a place where we value stuff that's handmade and hand-crafted. It's the wonder of bringing these inanimate objects to life in a beautiful way. We want to be a company where we tell interesting, unique stories with bold, innovative design and incredible artistry."

Henry Selick's first film at LAIKA was the eight-minute computer-animated *Moongirl* (2005), which had its origins in a contest at the studio for someone to create an idea for a short film.

"Mike Berger, a CG modeler here, had come up with the core concept of a girl who operates the moon," explains Selick. "His idea was chosen by Phil Knight and, after pitching my take of what I would do with it, I was hired to direct the short."

Selick wanted to create a new myth for children, with a *Twilight Zone* twist at the end. After several attempts at the script, he came up with a story that everyone was happy with. He was also able to test the limits of computer animation at that time.

"I got to push design and lighting," explains the director, "which are things I love to do. A lot of CG tends to be 'clean.' That's what it does well. So we tried to add textures—dirt, tone, and good, clear design. Also in CG, people over-light. They blast light because they want to make sure you see everything perfectly clear all the time. I think

Behind-the-scenes detail of the web living room.

we had some more interesting lighting and a broader range. I also got to work with some really fine animators.

"In my mind, it's what *The Nightmare Before Christmas* did for stop-motion. We really took CG into a new arena in terms of camera moves, lighting, mood, and so forth. This, in a much smaller way being a short film and all, was a pretty bold step.

"It said, 'We're serious about story, we're serious about CG, but our films aren't going to look exactly like everyone else's.' It has a bold look that I think is very attractive."

Moongirl subsequently won the Short Film Special Jury Prize at the prestigious Ottawa International Animation Festival, and Selick adapted his story as a children's book for Candlewick Press, with illustrations by Peter Chan and Courtney Booker, two of the key artists who worked on the film. A DVD copy of the short movie was included with the volume.

"When Henry first joined the company," Travis Knight recalls, "the first project we worked on was *Moongirl*. That was fairly terrifying for me, because he is an icon for a stop-motion animator.

"On *Coraline,* I again had to prove myself and make sure that I earned his trust and belief in me. As the studio's first major in-house foray into features, there's a lot of pressure on a lot of levels to make sure this thing is as beautiful as can be."

"I think *Coraline* is perfect for stop-motion," says Neil Gaiman. "It is such an interesting medium, because there is a solidity to stop-motion. It combines the control of animation with a reality, but you can also stylize that reality. For me, this is just perfect."

Principal animation finally got under way in March 2007. As with a live-action movie, the shooting of *Coraline* was divided into individual sequences that were usually grouped by the location of the scenes.

"Using these miniature puppets, miniature props, miniature sets, a complete world is brought to life by our animators," explains Henry Selick.

"I didn't realize until I visited the sets out in Oregon that absolutely everything you see on the screen somebody had to make," confesses Neil Gaiman. "Every blade

of grass had to be painted or built. They had rooms where they were just painting trees. If we see it, then somebody made it on a tiny, tiny scale—I also hadn't realized how small everything was.

"Everything had to be thought out. It all had to be designed and signed off on. It's astonishing."

Every element in each frame of *Coraline* was created and posed by hand. Shooting twenty-four frames per second, it took an entire week to complete just seventy-four seconds of footage.

"A puppet for stop-motion animation has to have some framework that will hold it up so that a human animator can manipulate that puppet and make it move," explains character fabrication supervisor Georgina Hayns, who was one of the first crew members to be hired on the movie. "That framework usually has to be a metal framework. It can be wire, or it can be an armature—a ball-and-socket and hinge-jointed version of a human skeleton. With Coraline, she had a miniature skeleton in her.

"All of our puppets are made up of silicone and foam latex, and then inside they have a metal skeleton. So they can stand, and each movement that the puppet makes it can hold that movement so that a frame of film can be shot.

The third transformation of the web living room set.

Robb Kramer and Douglass Mitchell prepare the landscape for the real-world house.

OPPOSITE INSET

Aaron Jarrett dresses the real-world house landscape.

LEFT

Scenic artist Aaron Jarrett dresses tulips behind the scenes in the real-world garden.

BELOW

Behind the scenes, model-maker Robb Kramer dresses the real-world garden.

"Those puppets had to withstand a lot. Unlike marionette puppets—where everything is happening in the real time—stop-frame puppets have to last a long time. To film *Coraline* took probably around a year and a half to get all the footage, so one puppet had to last all that length of time."

To physically construct one of the puppets for *Coraline* took around three or four months for each individual puppet and involved ten or more people. However, it all began with the design process.

"You start off with concept artists who design the look of that puppet," explains Hayns, another British veteran of *Corpse Bride*. "Then you move on to a sculptor to turn that two-dimensional image into a three-dimensional object. Then you talk to the director to see what performance he wants from that puppet. And then you break down how you are going to make that puppet—is it going to have a replacement face? Is it going to be a mechanical face? There are different forms of facial animation.

"So there are many different questions that need to be answered. Once you have decided what facial animation you want, you then go down through the body of the puppet and you work out what materials you will need to make everything from. The sculptor then sculpts the parts and separates them off. Then we have a mold-maker, who has to make molds of all of those individual parts.

"We have a casting team, who will cast the materials that each puppet is going to be made from, and we have an armature team that builds the metal skeletons to go inside those puppets. So that's the first part of the process.

"We get a basic puppet and then we have to clothe it, we have to give it hair, and then we have to paint it."

On *Coraline,* Hayns headed up a department of more than seventy character fabricators, puppet wranglers, armaturists, mold-makers, character painters, costume designers and fabricators, and hair-and-wig fabricators. Also, for the first time, computer technology was used to enhance the established construction techniques.

"Some of the puppet forms that we made were modeled by a computer," Hayns reveals. "Then we had a 3-D printer, so that helped us

CORALINE'S
MOTHER

create some of the elements, so that it was not all down to one sculptor to produce these parts. We still had to mold them, and then clean up certain things, but the use of technology on *Coraline* was very interesting."

"Walking around the studio in Oregon, seeing the maquettes, the armatures, the models, seeing those huge and wonderful sets, I felt so guilty," Neil Gaiman admits. "I just made this stuff up.

"There were all these people working on it, they had rooms that were full of people painting things, and I kept feeling that I should be apologizing to them all. I just wanted to tell them that I didn't know it would be so much work."

"More than anybody else, I think he was probably the most nerve-racking person to see what we were doing," admits Hayns about the author's visit. "We had the producers, the press, and all the big distributors coming around, but it is Neil Gaiman's baby. We just hoped that we were visualizing it in the same way that he would visualize it. So when he smiled, we all smiled."

For the character of Coraline alone, the production team created around thirty different puppets, more than two hundred thousand distinct facial expressions, and nine changes of costume.

"With Coraline, her nine costumes weren't designed when I arrived," admits Hayns. "So I worked with the costume department and Henry, and we took a lot of reference of teenage fashions. Between myself, Henry, and

Tadahiro's concept designs for the Other Mother's costumes, inspired by 1800s, 1920s, and 1970s fashion.

Artist Chris Appelhans's concept for the Other Mother's transformation.

*Fabric swatches
for the Other
Mother's costumes
are mapped out
for reference.*

BELOW

*Costumes for
Coraline's mother
were mocked up
for review.*

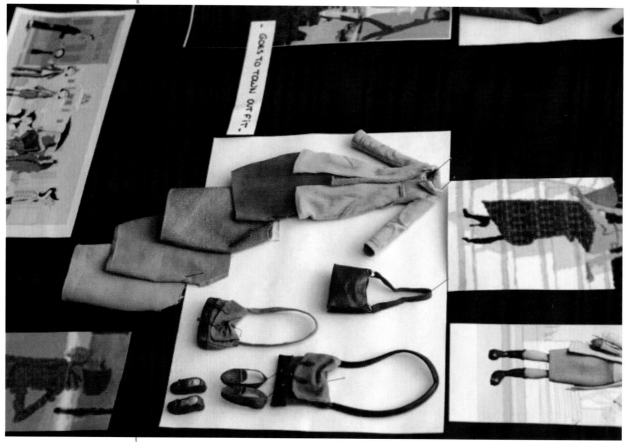

our costume designer, we came up with the look of her costumes, based on what was out there."

Firstly, a pattern would be made from the puppet, and then a mock-up of the costume would be created for review. Once Henry Selick had approved the shape and pattern, the costume department would modify the scaled-down garment and try out different materials.

"It took quite a few months to get each of the costumes together," lead costumer Deborah J. Cook explains. "We started with just images of regular clothing to see how we might want it to look. Then we researched fabrics. Then we did a lot of color and fabric tests."

"The costume department had to source the fabrics," adds Hayns, "because Coraline is nine-and-a-half-inches high. So, if you have a close-up of her on a big screen, you have to know that the scale of that fabric is going to look right on her. That

LEFT AND BELOW
Tadahiro's concept design for Coraline's rainy-day outfit was brought to life in the movie.

was challenging. My costume people went to Los Angeles, San Francisco, even London, trying to find the right materials."

In the end, the filmmakers had to silkscreen-print some of their own fabrics to create costumes from, just so the pattern conformed to the correct scale.

"Once we had the perfect shape," explains costume fabricator Elodie Massa-Allen, "then we had to duplicate, duplicate, duplicate. We always started with four or five duplicates, but when the animator worked with the puppets, they had to touch them thousands of times. So, often, four was not enough."

"If you have something really bright, shiny, and new, it's never going to stay that way," says Deborah Cook, who had previously worked as a puppet modeler on *Corpse Bride* in Britain. "So you'd get a little bit of dirt there to start with. And after the costume had actually been handled by the animators quite a lot, it settled around the puppet and the wear and tear happened naturally.

"When that got to be too much, we could repaint it, clean it up, coat it with something.

TOP

*T*adahiro's concept designs for Coraline's clothes.

ABOVE

*T*adahiro's concept designs for Coraline's pajamas.

RIGHT

*L*ead character painter Cynthia Starr puts the finishing touches to a twice-the-size puppet of the Cat.

LEFT

*H*air-and-wig fabricator Jessica Lynn carefully applies hair to the wig for the real mother puppet.

BELOW

A close-up view of Coraline's mother's hair.

We'd just make them fresh and start again. And if the costumes got a little too worn out, then we would just replace them."

Another challenge for the filmmakers was creating the hair for the puppets. For the first time in a stop-motion film, instead of using a sculpted hairpiece, director Henry Selick wanted the characters to look as if they had natural hair.

As a result, the production began experimenting with various types of animal hair and even very fine tinsel. "We started playing with different kinds of hair," recalls Georgina Hayns, "even real human hair. It was interesting. Henry wanted to see the movement of the real hair, but we couldn't do it. We tried everything. You find that human hair is too porous and does not want to stick to anything or do anything. So we ended up with a synthetic hair, which we laid on top of and underneath thin wires.

"For Coraline herself, we made four or five different stunt wigs for different actions that she goes through."

Lead hair-and-wig fabricator Suzanne Moulton not only had to devise a method that allowed the hair to remain firmly in place during the animation process, but she also had to come up with a way of keeping it clean.

ABOVE

*Coraline's star
sweater was used
in a number
of scenes over
several months of
shooting.*

BELOW

*Behind the scenes,
multiple versions
of Wybie's
telescopic mask
were finished
off in the paint
department.*

OPPOSITE

*After surprising
her in the orchard,
Wybie examines
Coraline through
his three-eyed
turret lens.*

"It goes through a lot of handling," she explains, "which is why we had replacement wigs. We did also have a process for cleaning them—a little drop of alcohol and a gentle hand."

The paint department had its own set of challenges to confront, as Hayns reveals: "Each part of the puppet has got paint on it. Even the costumes are painted into, so that they don't look brand new." Again, they worked very closely with Selick to show him step-by-step where they were going with the characters.

"That's where the maquettes were really useful, because we could use those as paint guides. We could give him a couple of options—light it, photograph it, see what it looked like on the screen and then move forward from there. We had a huge team of painters on board."

"We would just work out the color designs," explains character painter Joshua

Storey. "We would come up with a variety of different styles that we could show the director. He would then pick and choose, and sometimes he would choose aspects of each one and ask us to put them together."

In the end, Georgina Hayns admits that the most satisfying aspect of her work on *Coraline* was seeing those characters that started off as drawings come to life on the screen. "The most joyful part is when the animators would come in and say, 'Georgina, it's a great puppet. I love it.' Seeing that puppet come to life after all the hard work that goes into getting it to completion is great. It was absolutely so rewarding."

Coraline has the distinction of being the biggest production ever filmed in stop-motion to date.

"We had around thirty animators working on the film, give or take," reveals Henry Selick. "That's nearly twice as many as I've ever worked with before at one time."

More than one hundred and fifty different sets of varying sizes were hand-constructed at the LAIKA studios to depict the various locations required in the script. In fact, there were only about twenty setups in the film, but each set had to be replicated twice in different ways because they existed in both the real world and the Other World.

In many cases, test sets based on concept designs by Tadahiro were built and dressed with props. Then director of photography Pete Kozachik would light them and shoot some footage for Henry Selick and the crew to look at and make any adjustments and improvements that were considered necessary. Once everybody was happy, then the final reconfigured unit was put together for filming.

Maddy Gaiman accompanied her father on his tour of the studio facilities in February 2008. "It was amazingly super cool!" she recalls. "There were *so* many sets for all the different scenes in the movie.

"I imagined it would just be some little tiny sets, with people moving them a little bit at a time, as they do. But I didn't think that

Coraline first meets her Other Father in his study.

One of Tadahiro's concept designs for the Other Father's study.

it would be as elaborate as it was, or just how many sets there were. Some were built to little scales, but others were life-size and some were twice as big as that. They were huge. It was way cooler than I imagined."

According to set construction supervisor Bo Henry, although many of the props were utilized simply for set-dressing, others had to be constructed as mechanical pieces that could be used in conjunction with the stop-motion puppets.

For the more complex sets and props, a system of sliders, dials, motors, and needles with gauge marks would have to be incorporated into the design to allow the animators to know how far to move the multiple elements one frame at a time. These sets or props would have "tie-downs" built into them so that the puppet could be securely anchored with rods during the animation process.

"It's an area that allows the puppet to be mechanically fastened to the piece," Henry explains.

One such prop was Wybie Lovat's bicycle, which was an armature custom-made completely out of metal.

"There were a number of tie-downs on that," continues Henry. "It might be on a set for three months during the filming process, so it was a very deliberate process that every piece was pretty much handmade. On Wybie's bike, the exception was the sprockets and chains. We were able to find a buy-out element for that, which helped. It would have been a huge project to machine those pieces."

Some props were created using forced perspective to achieve a desired 3-D optical effect, while others were finished in a slightly cruder process to give them the illusion of little imperfections.

"The challenging part was to make a three-dimensional object look like an illustration," reveals British-born scenic artist Anthony Travis. "That's the whole look of the movie."

To create the bizarre blooms, pulsating plants, and telescopic topiary in the Other Mother's fantastic garden, animation rigger Oliver Jones utilized a wide variety of everyday materials, including Ping-Pong balls, lengths of wire, and various cylindrical objects.

One of the more unusual challenges for model-makers Rebecca Stillman and Kingman "K. C." Gallagher was creating a selection of lifelike cheeses out of rubbery silicone.

Even the flowered wallpaper design in Coraline's bedroom was hand-painted. The pattern was then enhanced using computer technology.

"In the book I could describe something indescribable," admits Neil Gaiman. "I could talk about walking through a fog, and the way that the trees stopped being trees and just became things that look like the idea of trees.

"That is something that you can do on paper, and it is something you can do in prose with somebody's imagination, because you know that nobody is ever going to have to draw it, or make it real.

"What was astonishing was watching them bring the book to life. They did it, and it is really quite disturbing in an incredibly cool way."

"It's taking different elements from all the arts to make something that is really unique and interesting," says lead animator Travis Knight. "We took a lot of processes from the theater, especially in the way that we built our sets and how we shaped and framed things."

Maddy Gaiman admits that she was surprised by some of the changes the production made. "I had always imagined the door to the Other World as a huge big door in a big, empty room," she explains. "A rather intimidating wooden door that was really hard for Coraline to open. Instead, it's a little door that she can crawl through. That was probably one of the main things that changed."

"I had never worked in a stop-motion studio before," Neil Gaiman reveals. "So it was a unique experience just for that. But it was also unique because I've been on many, many film sets over the years, and the atmosphere on a normal film set is a combination of weariness and excitement. For many people, it is a matter of trying to find things to do during the long periods where nothing is happening.

"One of the things that fascinated me about the stop-motion process is that there really were none of those long periods where nothing happened. Because somebody is moving something a fraction of an inch and it is actually incredibly important. Or someone else is repairing something, and another is making something.

OPPOSITE

Animator Teresa Drilling brings to life Tadahiro's concept designs of Coraline and the Cat's endless-walk sequence.

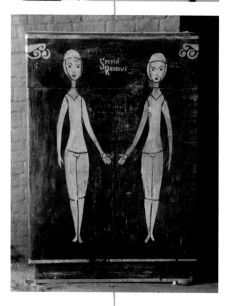

ABOVE

*P*rops on the kitchen set were built by hand.

CENTER LEFT

*E*very set detail of stop-motion film has to be made and applied into the set. From the larger props down to the magnets on the refrigerator, everything is designed and built. Linden's is named after Harry Linden, the line producer.

BOTTOM LEFT

*M*iss Spink and Miss Forcible's cabinet was built by hand and holds their old and sticky taffy.

RIGHT

*C*oraline puts seeds on the windowsill while she talks to her mother.

TOP RIGHT

Behind the scenes, animator Brad Schiff works through a hole cut under the bridge in the real-life garden. The animators sometimes had to get into tight or cramped positions to manipulate the shot.

RIGHT

Assistant animator Kent Burton manipulates the Other Father riding his Praying Mantis Tractor in the Other Garden.

FAR LEFT

*B*ehind the scenes, assistant animator Peg Serena works under the stage animating the rising pumpkins in the Other Garden.

LEFT

*M*odel-maker K.C. Gallagher demonstrates how some of the fantastic flowers bloom in the Other Garden.

BELOW

*T*he bleeding hearts in the fantastic garden.

OPPOSITE
TOP LEFT

*Animators
sometimes plan
out the path of
objects before they
shoot. In this
case, the path of
the refrigerator
door is marked
on the masking
tape. Each
mark represents
a frame of
animation. Many
of the marks
have a frame
number printed
next to them.*

OPPOSITE
TOP RIGHT

*Jeff Riley
animates the
Other Father
at the piano.*

OPPOSITE
BOTTOM

*The Other Father
sits at the piano
in the dark—
the result of Jeff
Riley's animation.*

"Making feature films is like war. Most of the people are standing around being cold and bored and waiting for the next moment of intense excitement and stress. Then it's all over, and you have to do it once again. There was none of that going on at LAIKA. Everything was happening—it was just happening very slowly. But it never, never stopped."

According to Travis Knight, "One of the exciting things for me about stop-motion is that it's the only form of animation that's dangerous on some level. Stop-motion is so immediate—you grab a puppet and pose it. Little things occur while you're out there, little accidents. To me, that's where a lot of the magic happens. You find this weird symbiotic relationship with this little doll.

"Stop-motion is probably the most stressful kind of animation. It's progressive—you start here, you end here, and that's it. You can't go back and change things, essentially. You can't mess up, so it's a little scary. There's always pressure, and there's always stress, but I think it helps you keep your edge."

"For most animation, you work out key poses," explains Henry Selick. "You time it out, and then assistant animators will 'in-between' those poses. CG animation is very similar, except you have a computer to help do the in-between poses."

While trying to come up with ideas for differentiating between the two worlds that Coraline exists in, the production originally looked at making one of the worlds stop-motion and creating the other using CG animation.

"We did some tests," reveals Travis Knight, "and ultimately decided that this story is perhaps better suited to stop-motion. I'm glad we went that way. We were going to have some fairly extensive CG effects, but again we decided this film would benefit from having a more hand-crafted look."

"I feel like Henry pushed the edge right now of what you can do with stop-motion," says Neil Gaiman. "Technically, it actually takes what you can do with stop-motion somewhere else."

"*Coraline* is an incredible opportunity to do something really unique in animation," says Knight. "You pinch yourself every morning that you had an opportunity to be part of something like this."

Although the techniques of stop-motion animation have essentially remained unchanged since the early days of cinema, for *Coraline* the animators at LAIKA reinvented the process to bring it into the digital age. Storing each frame on a computer allowed the animators to refer to a monitor while reviewing their previous shots. After checking the model with calipers, they would then move the puppet infinitesimally and then grab the next frame.

Knight readily admits that there is something paradoxical in combining an anachronistic film technique such as stop-motion animation with twenty-first-century technology.

Animator Chris Tootell behind the scenes on the orchard set.

Coraline: A Visual Companion

*The camera
lighting team:
Tim Taylor,
Chris Tootell,
James Wilder-
Hancock, and
Chris Peterson
(at back).*

RIGHT

*Coraline has
a conversation
with the Cat.*

"We've been able to figure out a way to take what's so great about the computer—which is really about capturing subtlety and refinement—and combining it with stop-motion, which is typically more crude.

"We shot with digital cameras. We captured everything digitally. Our frame grabs were all done with computers. You essentially can't do a stop-motion film without computers anymore, which is a weird thing."

"I love stop-motion," says animator Chris Tootell. "All the best texturing and rendering on CG, as good as it is, still feels different. We've come a long way, and there's a lot of great technology used nowadays—in the puppet armatures, in the facial expressions. It's not an old-school technology any longer—it's just another medium with which to tell a story."

On *Coraline,* the characters' different expressions were created using replacement animation. The puppets' faces were broken into two distinct sections—the brow shapes and the mouth shapes. When combined together, these brow and mouth shapes created the characters' full range of facial movements and expressions.

"There's an amazing amount of expression you can get from them," says Tootell. "There's a lot of freedom there for the animator."

"For facial animation, in particular," agrees Travis Knight, "we've been able to find ways to use a computer to help out the stop-motion. Replacement animation has been around forever, but there's only a certain amount of refinement you can get with it—it's hand-done and it's a little crude, but it does have a real beauty to it. With the computer you can make it pixel-perfect, get real subtlety.

"We have these machines that can transfer what we've done with the computer, make physical objects out of them. That's how we did a lot of the facial replacement animation. We were modeling and sculpting in the computer, printing them out on these wacky 3-D printers, painting them all by hand, and then fitting them and putting them on the puppets. That was how we got this really incredible, subtle, beautiful, and expressive facial animation."

In the finished film, Coraline herself has more than two hundred thousand different expressions.

"It hurts my stomach to think about all those poor people who had to paint all that stuff and build all that," says Knight. "But I think it shows. When you see the

RIGHT
Various expressions for Young Other Miss Forcible.

OPPOSITE
Just a few of Coraline's 200,000-plus different expressions.

film, she really does emote, and she feels like a real, living, breathing girl. Of course, all that comes from the animators."

Another of the thirty or so animators who worked on the film was Californian Amy Adamy, who describes her job as "Puppetry without strings." To animate one particular sequence in *Coraline,* involving the dancing mice, took Adamy sixty-six days of meticulous work in a darkened room.

"It was a dream sequence," she explains, "in which the Other Mother sends out her thoughts to Coraline to try to lure her through the door. There are floating mice—it's very psychedelic.

"I've never spent that long on a shot before, but it was just really difficult.

Everything was on strings. It was all connected, so that every time I would touch anything, something elsewhere started moving."

Adamy admits that the most difficult part of being an animator is trying to get the puppets' performance to convey everything that it should. "Sometimes," she says, "puppets are unwieldy. Things break, and you just have to not panic and fix it."

Because of the constant handling and moving of the puppets during production, such areas as the physical extremities or material with wires in it had a tendency to break on occasions. As a result, a puppet "hospital" was set up with a representative from each department in puppet fabrication on hand to make repairs on set or after a sequence was completed.

"Other animators know what you go through," continues Adamy, "and if they tell you that they like a particular shot, then it's a nice feeling to be appreciated."

After Coraline first chases a hopping Kangaroo Mouse through the small door behind the wallpaper, she crawls down a dark, expanding tunnel until she finds herself in an oddly different mirror world.

"And waiting for her there is her Other Mother," reveals Neil Gaiman. "And her Other Mother is a lot like the one that she left behind, only she has black buttons for eyes."

Later, however, the Other Mother and Other Father tell Coraline that if she wants to stay with them in the Other World forever, then she will have to sew a pair of shiny black buttons into her own eyes.

"There were a lot of things in the book which I wondered how Henry would do

ABOVE

Animator Amy Adamy poses a flat mouse for the mice dream sequence.

BELOW

The Other Mr. Bobinsky's jumping mice change their positions as they perform for Coraline.

ABOVE

The Other Mother, Other Father, and Other Wybie watch Coraline as she drifts to sleep.

RIGHT

The Other Mother and Other Father give Caroline a small box containing a spool of black thread, a silver needle, and a pair of shiny black buttons— for Coraline's eyes!

them," says Gaiman. "One of the simplest things, which was also one of the coolest and most disturbing, is the buttons for eyes. That is something that is very easy to say in a book—you just write that her eyes were buttons, and you figure that it will work, because you've seen dolls with buttons for eyes and you think that is a bit disturbing.

"But you haven't really thought it through. And then you go to the studio and you watch an entire world in which people have buttons for eyes. Henry's actually made it real, and it doesn't look silly. It looks slightly off, and it looks more and more disturbing. And I love that."

While she is exploring the Other World, Coraline discovers that Miss Spink and Miss Forcible's Other Apartment contains an enormous theater with a high wooden stage and rows and rows of seats occupied by button-eyed Scottie dogs.

"It was one of the coolest sets I was lucky enough to work on," says lead animator Eric Leighton.

For this sequence, 450 individual Other Scottie dogs were created. The background dogs were operated on a mechanical cam system, attached to cranks that could be controlled by hand to move the figures in a preset pattern. Those dogs featured in the foreground were wire-puppets that could be individually animated, as was a Scottie dog holding a flashlight in its mouth, who acts as an usher, showing Coraline down the aisle to her seat.

"I love the Scottie dogs," admits Gaiman. "I just love how many of them there are. The sheer number of them just made me incredibly happy.

"Every one of those little dogs could be moved up and down in their seats or brought forward or backward. They are all moving while there is proper flying-trapeze stuff going on. That just left me astonished.

"The Scottie dogs were one of the things that I stole from real life. In many ways, *Coraline* was jigsaw-puzzled together from little moments and incidents in my life. The Scottie dogs came from a Miss Webster and her partner. They were *theatrical* ladies of a certain age, and Miss Webster taught me elocution.

"Much like Miss Forcible, she had these massive bosoms, which she would fold her arms over. And they had this whole collection of little Scottie dogs with names like Jock, and Hamish, and Angus, who would follow them everywhere, barking.

"I just simply stole that for the book and had them living downstairs."

The author also recalls an earlier visit to the LAIKA studios, while tests were still being shot, when a problem arose about the original design of the Other Mother. "More than any other character, she changes throughout the story," Gaiman explains, "getting scarier and scarier-looking.

With the Other World she created literally disintegrating around her, the Other Mother finally reveals her true form to Coraline. Growing to twelve feet tall, she is

A theater full of button-eyed Scottie Dogs eagerly await the performance by the Other Miss Spink and Other Miss Forcible to begin.

withered to the bone. She has platelike shoulders and hips, with an arachnid's tail section. And her long, sharp fingers are made of needles.

As head story-artist Chris Butler explains, "The Other Mother goes through the most changes in the movie. In the final change, she is revealed as the monster that she really is, which is pretty horrific.

"She has a bug face. Down below, she has four legs. She is part-witch, part-insect at that point."

While trying to grab at an escaping Coraline, the beldam's wire-thin wrist is caught in the little door and her hand snaps off. Later, after Coraline has returned to the real world, she is attacked by the Other Mother's dismembered hand, which has a life of its own and scrambles after her with fingers that look like spider's legs.

"They were made of real silver," explains Amy Adamy, who was assigned the job of animating the Other Mother's terrifying needle hands, "very pointy and sharp. They were very expensive to make and very, very delicate."

Coraline is the first stop-motion feature film to be shot entirely in stereoscopic 3-D.

Although the first 3-D stop-motion film is considered to be John Norling's short film *In Tune with Tomorrow*, which was initially produced for the Chrysler exhibit at the 1939 New York World Fair, very little had been done with combining the process with animation until Disney's successful reissue of *Tim Burton's Nightmare Before Christmas* in a computer-generated 3-D format in 2006.

"What they did with the 3-D in *Nightmare* so well," explains Selick, "is they didn't oversell it.

"In the story of Coraline, she lives an ordinary life, albeit one that she's pretty unhappy with. Then she discovers a better version of that life, with a similar mother and father, a similar house, similar neighbors. But everything's improved.

"So, going back to *The Wizard of Oz* for inspiration, I was looking for a visual, dramatic device that would allow us to differentiate those two worlds.

"One of the most amazing things in *The Wizard of Oz,* especially when it first came out, was that this fantasy world Dorothy wakes up in is in color. She comes from a black-and-white world on the farm to this world full of magic. I needed an equivalent of that for Coraline.

"Well, *The Wizard of Oz* did it with color and, in its day, that was a relatively new thing. We are using new 3-D technology and the advent of digital projection in this new theater format to bring 3-D to our film.

"So, when Coraline leaves her compacted, claustrophobic, colorless life and goes through a secret door into the Other World, each of those places she thinks she knows is expanded and dimensional and rich and gives you a sense of breathing room."

"I usually hate 3-D," confesses Neil Gaiman, whose adaptation of *Beowulf* was widely released in the process in 2008. "I always put on my spectacles, and I look at things and go: well, I *guess* it looks 3-D. I know that the brain is meant to process these two images and create a 3-D effect of something coming out of the screen at me, but mostly it looks like two images on a screen at the same time.

"So normally, halfway through the movie, I take the glasses off. I'm irritated anyway, and then I put them back on.

"But the first time I saw a 3-D test on *Coraline,* my jaw just dropped. I didn't think I had ever seen any 3-D that looked that good. There is a genuine sense of reality that allows the film to get really scary in a way that a live-action *Coraline* movie would, frankly, simply keep the audience awake at night. And that would be a bad thing."

"When I directed my previous stop-motion films, *The Nightmare Before Christmas* and *James and the Giant Peach,*" reveals Selick, "I was aware of this magic on the set with these miniature puppets that were brought to life by our animators. But there was a magic there that could not be captured on film, because, in the end, the film was a flat, two-dimensional image.

"At that time we had a few people experimenting with taking 3-D or stereoscopic pictures, just like the old View-Masters—where you click through the images and you get some depth to them.

"Now there is digital projection and a new stereoscopic-glasses system that really is a much more comfortable, amazing experience. I'm friends with Lenny Lipton, who is at the forefront of that technology and who works at a company called Real D. Every few years I have been checking in with him.

"Then, three years ago, I saw his latest advances in stereoscopic imagery and I found the answer to my problem of differentiating the two worlds that Coraline lives in—the ordinary world and the wonderful, other version of her life."

Born in Brooklyn, New York, in 1940, Lipton had an independent income from song royalties (when he was nineteen years old, he wrote the lyrics to "Puff the Magic Dragon" while in college) and his book about independent filmmaking, which remained in print for twenty years. Then, in 1972, he decided that his calling was stereoscopic imaging, which had interested him since the age of ten, and he has since become the most prolific inventor in the field.

"A change has taken place in the way some stereographers look at the most basic aspect of stereoscopic composition," says Lipton, who has been granted thirty patents in the area of stereoscopic displays. "This change made its appearance only a few years ago. It provides what could well be described by that tired cliché as a paradigm shift. It's a new way of looking at the world of stereoscopic composition."

Real D Cinema is a high-resolution digital-projection technology that does not require two projectors, unlike the older 3-D projection processes. Real D uses a single

projector that alternately projects the right-eye frame and then the left-eye frame. Each frame is projected three times at a very high frame-rate, which reduces flicker and makes the image appear to be continuous. When viewed through circularly polarized glasses, which allow each eye to see only its "own" image, the result is a seamless 3-D picture that appears to extend in front and behind the projection screen.

"Very few people know how to do good cinema stereo photography," Lipton explains, "so I am spending some time working with the major film studios to get their creative people up to speed. I love that part of the job."

Although Lipton was brought into LAIKA to give a series of lectures to the film-makers about how the new stereoscopic technology affected every aspect of the production, Henry Selick admits that while shooting Coraline in 3-D, the production

Coraline proposes a game to the Other Mother.

The Movie   117

LEFT

The Other Mother's severed hand follows Coraline through the orchard.

TOP

The Other Mother confronts Coraline at the end of the game.

ABOVE

The Other Mother unlocks the little door.

was learning as it went along: "We would capture the essence of these miniature worlds and sets by shooting two pictures for each frame—a left-eye frame and a right-eye frame.

"You normally set the distance between the lens, when you are shooting a 3-D movie, at what human eye-level distance is," he continues. "But because we were shooting miniature puppets, we made the distance very, very slight."

Among those films so far shown in Real D are Walt Disney's *Chicken Little* (2005) and *Meet the Robinsons* (2007), *Monster House* (2006), *Beowulf,* coscripted by Neil Gaiman, *Journey to the Center of the Earth* (2008), and the reissue of *The Nightmare Before Christmas.*

"To the best of my knowledge, *Coraline* is the first stop-motion feature shot in 3-D," says Selick. "The technology of 3-D filmmaking has been around since the 1950s in some form or another. It went away for a while, but now it's back because it is much improved. They now prefer to call the process 'stereoscopy.' It's a way of just looking at things with both eyes as we're designed to do, which gives us depth perception.

"Real D captures the complete miniature stop-motion world that we, the filmmakers, had been aware of but have never really been able to share with our audience. So with *Coraline* we are going to use 3-D to bring them inside the worlds that we create.

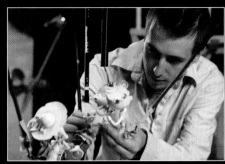

OPPOSITE

The three ghost children ask Coraline to find their eyes.

LEFT

Behind the scenes, Chris Tootell animates the three ghost children.

BELOW

Coraline finds herself imprisoned in the closet with the three ghost children.

"We are not relying on a lot of 3-D gimmicks, with things flying off the screen all the time. We use some of that, but use it very, very well. The 3-D experience will bring Coraline's story of the two worlds to life better than any other technique."

The filmmakers did not just rely on the 3-D effects to differentiate between the two worlds in *Coraline*. As Selick reveals, they also used other, more subtle techniques to convince the audience that they had crossed from one world into another. "The difference between the worlds is also a little bit about color," he reveals.

"We actually took the world that Coraline lives in, the sets, and crushed them as if her life is claustrophobic. The color's drained out. Her life feels flat.

"When she goes to the Other World, we recreated some of those same sets, but we built them deep and we shot them dimensionally. We also toned up the color a bit. And we moved the camera.

"In her real life, the camera's always locked and it's like a series of tableaus. Her real life feels like a stage play. But the Other World feels real, a place where you can breathe."

"Henry's incredible," says lead animator Travis Knight. "He started out as an animator, so that is in his blood. He has that incredible visual sense. He understands motion, and movement, and acting, better than anyone I've ever worked with. He makes the

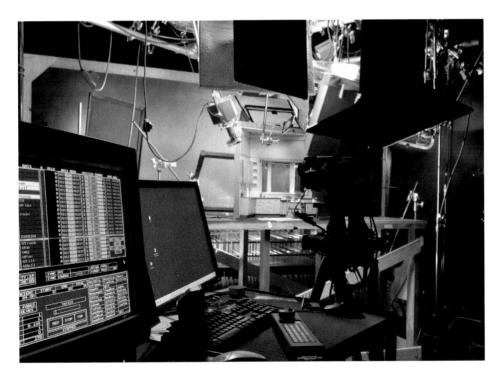

OPPOSITE TOP LEFT
Behind-the-scenes shot of the theater set.

OPPOSITE TOP RIGHT
Animator Teresa Drilling animates the Other Forcible and Spink during their trapeze show.

OPPOSITE
The younger versions of the Other Miss Forcible and the Other Miss Spink catch a falling Coraline at the climax of their performance.

ABOVE
The Redlake Camera system.

LEFT
Behind the scenes on the real-world kitchen set, with camera and computer equipment.

RIGHT

*Coraline's real
mother wants
her to eat her
vegetables.*

BELOW

*Coraline sees her
parents trapped
behind the hallway
mirror.*

OPPOSITE

*Coraline and
the Cat crouch
in broken mirror
shards.*

animators around him better. He can look at something and he can say, 'Shift that by four frames,' and he's exactly right.

"He is brilliant. He knows animation in and out, but he also brings an interesting and very unique point of view to things. His films are really unlike anything else. And I think *Coraline* really is the greatest thing that he's ever done. He's made some great films, but *Coraline* tops them all. It's very special."

"Henry has definitely got a strong vision," agrees animator Amy Adamy. "He doesn't compromise. Henry definitely wants to get what he's imagining up there on the screen. We'd act out shots together, or he would draw a picture to convey what he wanted. He just has an eye for animation.

"*Coraline* reminds me of the old German fairy tales. Where the little kid doesn't appreciate anything and they get punished horribly. Obviously, Coraline prevails and protects her parents. I think she learns to appreciate that things may not always be perfect, and she grows and develops into a more complete person."

"*Coraline* is very innovative," confirms character-fabricator Georgina Hayns, "and Henry is responsible for that. He could have been the puppet-maker on this. He could have been the art director on this. He could have been the head of set construction on it.

"Henry is a very, very creative person, so he's always pushing the boundaries—going off down avenues you'd never believe, and trusting the solutions that are put in front of him. That might seem crazy, but he would actually go along with it and just say, 'Well, let's see what it looks like.' *Coraline* was definitely a very innovative production to work on."

LEFT

Coraline and her Other Mother and Other Father at the Fantastic Dinner Table.

ABOVE

Behind the scenes, director Henry Selick inspects preliminary work done by the art department on one of the sets.

3

The Characters

We have teeth and we have tails.
We have tails we have eyes.
We were here before you fell.
You will be here when we rise.

"*Coraline* is a story that doesn't have lots and lots of characters," reveals director Henry Selick. "But although it's a smaller ensemble, we still have some amazing individuals, most of them created by Neil Gaiman."

Once actors had been cast in a specific role, they were then sent the script and their voice performance subsequently digitally recorded in a sound studio.

"Sometimes it's very challenging," explains Selick, "because they don't have sets or props or costumes. They are just doing the voice work, and you have to record numerous different versions so that you can change your mind later about what you need in a particular scene.

"So what we do is we record the voices first, and then we have someone read the sounds so we know where all the mouth positions should be. Then later, the animators match the puppets' mouth movements to the words that the actors have already recorded."

OPPOSITE

Wybie, Coraline, and the Cat regard each other with curiosity.

ABOVE

*Another of
Tadahiro's early
character designs
for Coraline.*

OPPOSITE

*Coraline finds
her way into
the Other Mr.
Bobinsky's attic.*

FOLLOWING
PAGES

*Coraline chases
hummingbirds
stealing her
looking stone.*

From the very beginning of the production process, the filmmakers at LAIKA were aware of how essential it was that each character not only looked exactly right on the screen but also that the actors voicing those characters were equally suited to their roles.

"When you go for stop-motion animation," Selick continues, "you try to get to the essence of each individual character. And then you exaggerate. However, you wouldn't want to make things too realistic, because then you would be better off shooting a live-action film.

"Also, when you voice a character in animation, you're really creating the heart of that character. The entire performance that the animator brings to that character is triggered from the vocal performance.

"Coraline Jones is our heroine. Her whole life she has been cursed with a name that people pronounce wrongly. So she's got a little chip on her shoulder to begin with. Every kid's got something about them that the adults around her don't get right. She's got the little name problem.

"Coraline is very appealing to me," says Selick, "and I hope that she will be very appealing to children for a variety of reasons. She's got an overwhelming curiosity. If she sees something interesting, then she has to know about it.

"But that's a small problem for her. She's a very curious and adventurous girl, who likes to think of herself as an explorer. She imagines worlds under rocks, behind secret doors, or over the next hill. She is someone who cannot be held back.

"Coraline is also very skeptical, especially of what adults tell her, as most kids should be. She wants to find out what's really going on. She is someone who is very brave and imaginative, but she's also very stubborn. Coraline can pretty much win any stubbornness contest.

"Unlike some girls, she's into more creepy things, which I think will appeal to boys. She collects old stuff, like rusty toys, and then makes them into art objects. She's a very creative girl."

In October 2005, the first actor announced as being attached to *Coraline* was Dakota Fanning in the pivotal role of eleven-year-old Coraline Jones.

Born in Georgia in February 1994, Hannah Dakota Fanning was cast at the age of five in a Tide commercial and appeared with R&B musician Ray Charles in a

television spot for the state lottery. This led to more commercials work and guest roles on NBC's long-running medical drama *ER*, Fox's *Ally McBeal,* and the CBS show *CSI: Crime Scene Investigation*.

"I've always wanted to be an actress," Fanning admits, "ever since I was a little girl. It's fun to know what I want to do when I grow up. I have friends who say, 'Oh, maybe I'll be an astronaut or whatever.' But it's cool to want to do this forever. I knew from my first commercial that I wanted to be an actress."

More guest appearances followed, and when the young actress costarred opposite

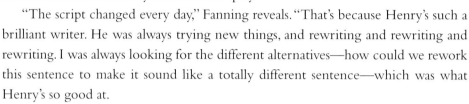

RIGHT
*M*ore of
Tadahiro's
character designs
for Coraline.

BELOW
*C*oraline
unknowingly
uses poison oak
as a dowsing
rod in the real
orchard.

Sean Penn in the film *I Am Sam* (2001), about a mentally challenged man fighting for custody of his seven-year-old daughter, she became the youngest person ever to be nominated for a Screen Actors Guild Award.

Before she recorded her character for *Coraline*, the young performer first read Neil Gaiman's original novel and then Henry Selick's screenplay.

"The script changed every day," Fanning reveals. "That's because Henry's such a brilliant writer. He was always trying new things, and rewriting and rewriting and rewriting. I was always looking for the different alternatives—how could we rework this sentence to make it sound like a totally different sentence—which was what Henry's so good at.

"Coraline finds a mysterious little door, which doesn't lead to anywhere because it's all bricked up. And then, in the middle of the night it mysteriously opens and there's a hallway to the Other World.

"It's such a real story of people thinking the grass is greener on the other side, and wanting something more than they have. That was so appealing to me.

"When you read the book, you fear for Coraline and just want her to get home. And in a way, you know she will. You have faith in her—that she's going to find a plan and, with the help of the cat, she's going to get home. But I think that when adults read it, they're seeing a little child lost, not being able to find her real parents."

"*Coraline* is the story of an ordinary girl who faces pure evil and triumphs," says Selick. "We are not going to soft-pedal the evil. It's going to be scary. But Coraline is much like some of the other heroes of modern family films—like Lucy Pevensie in *The Chronicles of Narnia: The Lion, the Witch and the Wardrobe,* or Hermione Granger in the *Harry Potter* films."

"Coraline reminds me of Dorothy in *The Wizard of Oz* and Alice in *Alice in Wonderland,*" observes Fanning. "They are very dark and scary stories, and *Coraline* also has some very scary and frightening elements.

"She is also a very adventurous girl—Coraline is always looking for adventure. She's also very curious, and she's a collector of things that most people would not even pay attention to. But those are Coraline's treasures. She loves bugs, and dirt, and mud, and just likes to go outside and get herself dirty."

Coraline is dismayed to discover that the little door opens onto a brick wall.

ABOVE

Coraline is frightened by the Other Father's impossible "long face."

LEFT

Coraline and the Cat watch as the mother/father doll burns in the fireplace.

"Coraline is a very independent character," adds Henry Selick, "very perceptive. So she's a great role model, but she is also someone who has imperfect parents. We all have imperfect parents. She is tempted by a much better version of her own life. However, in the end, she knows who she really loves, and is willing to risk her own life to rescue her imperfect parents."

Neil Gaiman agrees: "I love Coraline herself—she's just so full of vim and spunk and all those lovely old-fashioned words."

While Dakota Fanning was recording her dialogue for *Coraline*, the filmmakers also shot her performance on video, as the actress explains: "They were videoing me, so if there was anything I happened to do—a gesture or a facial expression—they could put that into Coraline's character. Because when you're doing a voice performance you don't have your body and your facial expressions to portray things, you have to really overdo it a little bit to get your point across.

"The first time that we recorded in the studio, they brought big pictures of some sets and all of the models—of the Other Mother, of the mother, of the Other Father, of the father, Mr. Bobinsky, Miss Spink and Miss Forcible, and Coraline, of course. And Henry had given me pictures of what the pink house was going to look like. So they had that for me the first couple times, which was so helpful and so nice.

"The trick with it was to be frightened and smart at the same time. Coraline's so scared, but she realizes she has to pull together and not let her fear overcome her. She knows that she has to come up with a plan to escape the Other World.

"Coraline really does get out of the situation herself, with help from others. She figures out how to use the rock with the hole in it, and how to trick the Other Mother. Ultimately, her plan does work out and she really can say that she did it. She figured it out herself. I think that can show other children watching the film that whatever their situation may be, whatever their problems may be at school or whatever, they can find a way out of it and make a better situation for themselves."

"Dakota is so good that you forget there's somebody playing Coraline," says Gaiman. "She has this little midwestern accent, which she doesn't usually have. You don't listen to her and think, 'That's Dakota Fanning.' You truly believe that she *is* Coraline."

"Dakota Fanning is a very gifted actor who brings great skill and emotional depth to the character," agrees Henry Selick, "and I can't think of anyone who would be better at playing Coraline. She's one of the best actors I've ever worked with. She understands the character. She makes Coraline believable.

"Coraline has to be able to stand up to almost anything, and Dakota brings that out in her performance of the character. It's not this false bravura.

"One of the most difficult things was to take a character who is actually bratty and self-centered, who doesn't think about others at the beginning of the film, and

ABOVE

Coraline returns through the passageway.

LEFT

Coraline knocks on Miss Forcible and Miss Spink's door.

make that character appealing. Dakota does that. Coraline is selfish. She's not happy about having moved. She can't see it from anyone else's perspective."

Neil Gaiman is quick to point out that, in his mind, the character in the movie doesn't look the same as the one he created for the novel.

"Henry's version of Coraline is totally different from how I originally imagined the character," admits the author, "but that's cool. The truth is, I'm not sure that I ever really had a clear idea of how she looked. In my head, I guess she looked like my daughter Holly. But she never really looked like Holly, because when I started writing it, Holly was around five years old, and I was imagining a girl who was nine or ten, somewhere around that.

"The truth is that I wasn't quite clear when I was writing it on how old she was. People would ask me how old Coraline is, and I would answer that she is the same age as Alice in *Alice in Wonderland*. That was because I thought that Alice didn't have an age, but then I looked in the book and I discovered that Alice is actually seven years old.

"I think that Coraline is probably a little bit older than that."

Dakota Fanning enjoyed the fact that there were elements of her character that she could personally identify with: "Coraline has blue hair and turquoise fingernails and clothes that I want," reveals the actress. "The clothes that she wears, I would wear in a second. For Christmas, Henry gave me a model of Coraline. Then, for my birthday, he gave me a little Coraline doll, one of the models. So I have those on our bookshelf, and I look at them every day. She has blue hair, a yellow raincoat, little striped tights, and swampers, as they call them in the movie. I call them galoshes, but they're like rain boots."

"Henry's Coraline has a wonderful little quirky mouth and pointy nose," says Gaiman, "and she stomps everywhere. She's really a lot like my youngest daughter Maddy was at that age—at the point where she suddenly stretched into a beanpole and her nose got long."

Although Maddy Gaiman is not sure that she agrees with her father's description of her, she does reveal that "The part that really reminds me of myself in the movie is where Coraline's father sings her the song that begins, 'Oh . . . my twitchy witchy girl.' That I can identify with. That was a song that my dad would sing to me when I was little. I definitely think of myself when I see that part of the movie, but I guess I see a little more of my sister Holly in Coraline."

"Yes, I would sing that to her when she was little," confirms her father. "It would make her laugh, but I have no idea where it came from."

"This whole experience has been really amazing," says Dakota Fanning, "and I'll always remember it. Henry Selick is really amazingly talented and so patient, and I don't think I could ever do what he does. I don't think anyone can be like him— he's absolutely incredible."

The key relationship in the movie is between Coraline and her mother, Mel Jones, and also between Coraline and her Other Mother, whom she meets in the Other World.

"Her real mom is a talented writer and leader of the family, especially when there's pressure," explains Henry Selick. "The family has just moved out to a new job in Oregon. They're behind schedule, and they were in a car accident on the way.

"Coraline's mom got whiplash. So she's under the gun. And she's not great at pretending to care about every little thing that Coraline wants or needs in this new life of hers. In fact, she's surprised, because when they were back home Coraline had her own friends.

"Coraline thinks her mom is awful, but she's like a lot of mothers. She can't always be shining and loving every moment. She has her bad days, and she knows what's

mother

LEFT

Tadahiro's character design for Coraline's mother.

BELOW

For most of the film, Coraline has a strained relationship with her mother, who is overworked and stressed.

important—which is keeping the family together and keeping it going, which a real mom is great at.

"Of course, in Coraline's view, she's not feeling anything from her real mom, because her mom doesn't have time for her right now. Then she discovers her Other Mother. Here's a woman who looks almost exactly like her real mom, but she's a little prettier. She cooks wonderful homemade meals for Coraline. She's planted a magical garden for Coraline. She wants to play games with her, be there for her, be her friend—all the things that Coraline thinks she would like her real mother to be."

"But then the Other Mother starts to waste away more and more," adds Dakota Fanning, "and she becomes more witchlike."

Eventually, in May 2006, the producers, with Selick's approval, cast Teri Hatcher in the dual role of Coraline's mother and the increasingly frightening Other Mother. Born in Palo Alto, California, in December 1964, the Golden Globe–winning actress is best known for her roles as the Man of Steel's girlfriend, Lois Lane, in the ABC-TV series *Lois & Clark: The New Adventures of Superman* (1993–97), and the hapless divorcée Susan Mayer in the same network's smash hit show *Desperate Housewives* (2004–present).

Hatcher confirms that Coraline's mother is under a lot of pressure and not particularly sympathetic when the audience first encounters her. "I think it's really clear," she says.

"They have just moved, she's under a deadline, she's got her neck in a brace, it's raining, it's muddy, nothing's going right. Ultimately you do see that this is a mother who loves her child, but it's also a mom who's reached the end of her rope."

"Teri Hatcher is absolutely amazing," says Neil Gaiman. "She plays the different mothers—the slightly grumpy, natural, real-world mother, and then the variants on the Other Mother. She goes from this incredibly sweet, attractive character all the way through to the how-scary-can-you-get one. She's astonishing."

"I play three different voices, the three different versions of the same character," explains Hatcher. "I play the mother who is really tired and worn out. I think a lot of moms will relate to her. She's got a lot of pressure on her, but she's a good person.

"Then there's the Other Mother, who is just surreally perfect and can do anything for you. She's the most perfect mom anybody would ever want. She's the perfect cook and has the perfect answer to any question. And Coraline really starts to think that this Other Mother is better than her old, tired mother.

"And then I play what I call the Evil Mother, which is really when the Other Mother starts to not get her way. Her true colors are revealed, and she becomes quite

The Other Mother encourages Other Wybie to keep smiling.

RIGHT

The Other
Mother presents
the button eyes
to Coraline.

BELOW

More of
Tadahiro's
numerous
character designs
for Coraline's
Other Mother.

OPPOSITE

The Other
Mother agrees
to play a game
with Coraline.
If Coraline can
find the eyes
of the ghost
children and
discover the
whereabouts of
her parents, then
everybody will
be allowed to
go free.

FOLLOWING
PAGES

The Other
Mother waits
for Coraline
in the "bug"
living room.

monstrous. She's an evil force that has existed for many, many years. Coraline is not her first victim, and she thrives on the souls of children."

"The way I like to go about casting voices," reveals Henry Selick, "is we knew we had Dakota Fanning as the central voice. So I literally cut at least fifty to seventy other actresses' voices against Dakota Fanning. And Teri Hatcher was right at the top of our list. It felt right."

"I just adore Henry," says Hatcher. "He's a fascinating accumulation of different kinds of personality traits. He can be very quiet, very mannered, and very specific about what his vision is. But he's so supportive. He really will take the time to communicate to you just the subtle line-reading he's looking for. Then, on top of that, he gives you the freedom to try something different. He has no inhibitions about saying, 'That was great and I didn't expect that,' or 'I hadn't thought of that.'

"He's so smart, you can just see the passion he has for this project. He's worked so hard on it, and he's such a lovely, lovely man."

"Of course, Teri loved the challenge," explains Selick. "She has this sexy, warm, beautiful instrument of a voice, but she also had to be a bitch. That's how Coraline sees her mom in the film, and we

have to understand why Coraline would pull away. And then when Teri plays the Other Mother, it's just warm and inviting. Of course you would want to hang out with her. So it's great to see her play these versions of the same character."

"Approaching the three characters was really challenging and a lot of fun," confirms the actress. "The way that I approached each one was that I tried to relate that woman to me.

"I've known mothers—myself included—who are tired and had it, but still love their children. So that's where that came from. The Other Mother was interesting, because we wanted her to be real, but *more so*. She had to be that person who can lure someone in with the candy.

"For Evil Mom I had to let the inhibitions go. I was just standing in the recording studio and *screaming* into the microphone. She was such fun to do, but it was also intimidating.

"When I started, I didn't know what anyone would want. However, as the process evolved, I became more confident in being more humorous, or more sarcastic, or more evil. As they cut scenes together they would realize, 'We need this to be scarier than we thought at first.' So they would record a lot of different takes, and then they would put it all together and make it work.

"It's amazing how the animators can take your voice and just pick up every little inflection and combine it with the puppet to make it look so real.

"It's been something of an amazing journey. When I first started working with Henry, I had no idea how long animated films took to finish. I've been doing this for two years, and Henry and his team have been working on it for more than five years.

"So much passion and such commitment goes into these projects, and I have loved working with these people. My daughter and I were lucky enough to be able

to go up to Portland and see the sound stages where all the animation was being created. It is an unbelievable level of artistic genius—all these craftsmen who can create these puppets and move them a tiny bit, frame by frame. It's just magnificent."

"While some might not admit it," reveals Henry Selick, "Coraline's Other Mother is really sexy. But she goes through these stages, and she ultimately turns out to be quite evil.

"We tried it in different ways, and it turned out that when Teri pulled back and quieted down, it became incredibly scary.

"This other mother also evolves. At first, Coraline's Other Mother is like a spitting image of her real mother—except her hair is clean and styled, and her clothes aren't worn and baggy. She stands a little taller, and has more energy, and she takes an interest in Coraline. But every time that Coraline goes back to the Other World, her Other Mother seems a little more beautiful. In fact, she is transforming. She is becoming this ideal version of Coraline's real mother, or at least what Coraline thinks would be the very best version of her mother.

"But then, one day, Coraline makes the Other Mother very angry, and then that evolution takes a wrong turn and she grows before Coraline's eyes into a freakish, scary version, who is very powerful and incredibly strong. And that is when she grabs Coraline and drags her to the closet and locks her in with the other ghost children. She can stay in there until she learns good manners and how to be a loving daughter. And it only gets worse from there . . ."

Teri Hatcher explains that she put a lot of herself into the character she plays. "I feel very attached to her," says the actress. "I see myself as a mother, so I feel like I created her. She even looks a little like me. Henry's a really great director in that he knows what he wants, but he also loves it when you surprise him.

"I loved the challenge of the range of the voice, that was pretty amazing. I loved getting to work with Henry—I'm such a big fan of *The Nightmare Before Christmas*."

Neil Gaiman was also particularly pleased with the way the character turned out on screen: "Watching what Henry's done with the Other Mother, and her gradual transformation, is an absolute delight," he says. "Teri Hatcher, more than anyone, has to play a number of different parts, and she's really good."

"My young daughter, Emerson," says Teri Hatcher, "looked at some of the preliminary artwork and she said, 'You have to do this movie.' A lot of celebrities want to do movies that their kids will ultimately enjoy."

In fact, it turned out that Emerson Hatcher also has a small voice role in *Coraline,* as her mother reveals: "I am very hesitant about Emerson being in front of the camera. I want her to be anything but an actress. We try to keep our private life as private as you can in this business, but she had read the script and she asked if she could be one of the voices.

"So Henry had her audition on the phone. She sat in my bedroom on the phone and he was up in Portland, and he just talked to her and would say, 'Tell me about yourself,' so she would start telling him. And somehow he got her to start doing this really, really cute voice.

"So she did that, and she did a few other things to the point where she seemed comfortable. So he had her play a Magic Dragonfly in the film. She was very excited. She went to the recording studio and he just talked her through it. She has a few lines and sounds. It's a very small part, but she's excited to be in it."

"Coraline's downstairs neighbors," Henry Selick explains, "are these two old English actresses, Miss Spink and Miss Forcible, who live in a fantasy world of their past, thinking they were great actresses when probably they were music-hall queens."

In fact, Neil Gaiman based the two elderly thespians on his childhood elocution teacher and her partner. "She had these magnificent bosoms," he recalls, "and the little Scottie dogs."

"They're warm, and friendly," says Selick, "and a bit full of themselves. At least, Miss Forcible is, because she's still always on stage and overacting and very *dramatic*."

When the filmmakers initially began discussing casting the voices for Miss April Spink and Miss Miriam Forcible, author Neil Gaiman decided to get involved in the process. "I only had one big casting suggestion," he reveals, "which Henry acted upon, and which made me feel very important, frankly. That was having French and Saunders doing Miss Spink and Miss Forcible, because Dawn French had read the English audiobook of *Coraline* and had done such an amazing job of it.

"I was listening to it and it got up to the part where Coraline is trapped in the darkness with the three ghost children, and I'm sitting there scared. And I thought, 'Why am I scared? I wrote this. I know what happens next.' But listening to Dawn—she has just this

spink　　　forcible

Tadahiro's early character design for Miss Spink and Miss Forcible.

lovely, warm, friendly voice and it draws you in and you feel comfortable and enveloped. And at the point where it's scary, it is somehow so much *more* scary."

When Coraline discovers the downstairs theater in the Other World, velvet curtains open to reveal a seaside setting with rotating waves and a cutout ship. The Other Miss Spink and Miss Forcible rise up out of the stage in mermaid outfits and sing a song, competing with each other for the most enthusiastic reaction from the audience of rowdy, button-eyed Scottie dogs.

Then the two old troupers unzip their fat-suit disguises, and their younger selves emerge in sexy bathing costumes. They proceed to swing through the air on matching trapeze bars, tossing a delighted Coraline between them.

"At one point Miss Spink and Miss Forcible are revealed in their younger days, in their glory," Selick confirms. "At first they are the same old ladies, but they're performing dangerous stunts on stage. Then they unzip fat suits and step out as their younger, beautiful selves.

MISS SPINK & FORCIBLE

"So I wanted to use the same voices for both the older and younger characters. There are a couple of British comedians, Dawn French and Jennifer Saunders, who have been a comic team for a number of years. They're friends with Neil Gaiman. French and Saunders are one of the outstanding comedy duos in the world, and incredible character actors."

Welsh actress and comedienne Dawn French was born in October 1957. While studying at London's Central School of Speech and Drama in 1977, she met her future comedy partner Jennifer Saunders.

Another of Tadahiro's character designs for Miss Spink and Miss Forcible.

Coincidentally, both women had grown up on the same Royal Air Force base on the island of Anglesey, Wales. However, despite having had the same best friend, the pair never met until later, when reportedly they initially loathed each other.

Despite their mutual dislike of the other, they eventually ended up sharing a flat together in North London while at college. Following graduation, French and Saunders formed a stand-up comedy double act, but it was not until they joined U.K. alternative-comedy collective The Comic Strip in the early 1980s that they came to the attention of the general public.

In 1987 the duo launched their own comedy sketch show, *French & Saunders,* on BBC 2. It proved to be a huge success, and in the early 1990s the program had the highest budget in BBC history.

While the pair continues to work together, they have also had huge individual successes—Saunders with the Emmy and BAFTA Award–winning series *Absolutely Fabulous* (1992–96; 2001–05), which she wrote and starred in, and French as the

ABOVE

*M*iss Spink and
Miss Forcible in
their basement
apartment.

LEFT

*M*iss Spink and
Miss Forcible's
Scottie Dogs
crowd the sofa.

OTHER MISS SPINK & FORCIBLE

RIGHT AND BELOW

Tadahiro's character designs for the Other Miss Spink and Other Miss Forcible's stage performance.

OPPOSITE

The Other Miss Spink is "practically naked" as she rises from the stage dressed in a mermaid suit.

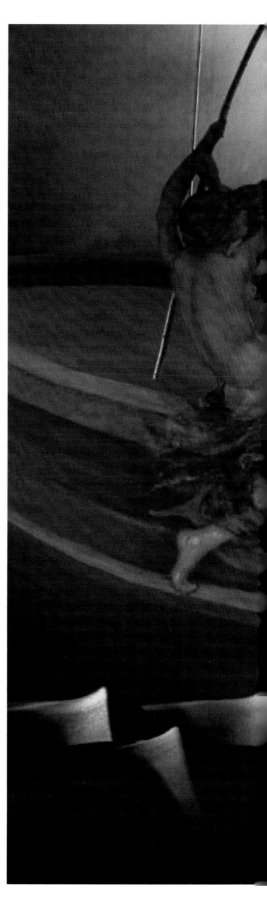

star of the long-running *The Vicar of Dibley* (1994–2007), created by Richard Curtis.

"I said to Neil that I would love to get involved in this film one way or the other," recalls Dawn French, "although an awful lot has changed. The original book is very different from the film, but in a good way."

"I think Neil's specialty is actually thinking up really truly dreadful things that you could not even imagine yourself," says Jennifer Saunders. "Something about the button eyes is really, really sinister."

To record the two actresses' voice performances, director Henry Selick traveled to London, but things did not go as smoothly as everyone hoped. "Everything was prepared," he recalls, "and they were assigned their parts. We spent a whole day with Dawn French playing Miss

RIGHT

*T*adahiro's concept design for the Young
Other Miss Spink and Miss Forcible
emerging from their fat suit disguises.

BELOW

*T*he Young Other Miss Spink
emerges from her fat suit.

Spink and with Jennifer Saunders doing Miss Forcible. At the end of the day it was good, but it wasn't great.

"So I reversed their roles. There are a lot of actors who would have just walked out of the room. They just took a breath, nodded their heads, and said they would try it. And so they switched parts. From then on everything was great."

Although it is usual with animated films to record each voice individually, Selick decided to make an exception with the two actresses and record them together in the studio.

"That really worked with French and Saunders," he explains, "because they've been a team for much of their professional careers."

"The funny thing is that because we work together an awful lot, you almost become one person," reveals Saunders. "Even when Henry first called me up, I said, 'I don't understand which one I'm playing,' because we are strangely interchangeable."

"We are quite often just the flip sides of a coin of the same person," French agrees. "That is often what we tend to do. Even if we decide that we are playing different characters, we get to whatever the job is and suddenly the voices become one voice.

"I think a lot of working up character for voices is about trust, actually. Trusting the director, and trusting the writer. Trusting the other person, and being open to suggestions and trying something different.

"I think Miss Forcible is the more theatrical in a funny way. It's odd really, because originally Henry had said to me that he thought my character might have a lighter voice because I think he wanted her to be sweeter. But in fact I have a much deeper voice than Jennifer."

"When we first came in," interjects Saunders, "it was going to be the other way around and I was going to be the lower, slightly more commanding voice. Then Henry asked for a little bit of sexiness to come in. There are lines that are very dramatic, where they are thinking about becoming performers again, and there are lines where Miss Spink puts a bit of sexy innuendo into it.

"It was lovely working with Henry. He gives you a lot of confidence. You always think it will be a bit pedantic to go over and over a line, but it's really interesting and you discover a lot more about the character. Normally if we are working on something together, we tend to go for one kind of choice because it's the choice that fits our natural rhythms. It was interesting to try other rhythms and other volume levels."

The Young Other Miss Spink and Miss Forcible as conceived by Tadahiro.

ABOVE

Miss Spink introduces Coraline to her collection of deceased Scottie Dogs.

RIGHT

Tadahiro's character designs for Miss Spink.

"What is interesting for me," adds French, "is that Henry is American, and so I don't know how much he knew about what we have done for the last twenty-five years together. That was quite refreshing, really. Because we didn't know what he knew, we didn't know what he expected. We came to please. What I really liked was that he was open to suggestions, and that is a rare thing and a good thing."

"They both had a great challenge and they rose to it," confirms Selick, "shedding the years in their vocal performances. And they're funny as hell. They're scary funny."

"I think Miss Spink and Miss Forcible have a habitual bickering that happens often with older people," says Saunders. "You notice it when your parents get a bit older. One person says one thing, and the other has to disagree. They simply can't agree.

"They are not being horrible to each other, it's just a force of habit. I think that they bicker, bicker, and bicker. I think Miss Forcible treats Miss Spink as a bit of a doormat, but she is the one that will do things. She can be a little more hysterical because Miss Spink is the more grounded of the two."

"I think Miss Spink is very fond of Miss Forcible," says French, "she probably thinks that she was quite a glamour-puss and remembers that. Also, she may possibly be a little jealous. Miss Spink is aware that Miss Forcible doesn't have a lot going on in the brain sometimes."

"It's more a *What Ever Happened to Baby Jane?* rivalry," observes Saunders

"That's very funny," agrees French, "I like that in the script. I like them trying to top each other, even in the song they try to get up an octave to prove that one is better than the other.

"I've got a feeling that Neil put these two characters in there so that Coraline can have some friends. Or people that she might need. I know she has Wybie, but she might also need some adults that she can rely on a little bit and that are good fun. I think she needs them. She needs a little bit of guidance. She needs the luck that they give her with the stone, and I think they are a comfort in a way."

Tadahiro's various character designs for Miss Forcible's costumes.

ABOVE AND RIGHT

*T*adahiro's concept designs for the
Other Miss Spink and the Other
Miss Forcible's theatrical costumes.

BELOW

*M*iss Spink and Miss Forcible argue
over Coraline's tea leaf reading.

Coraline: A Visual Companion

*M*iss Spink
attacks the old
and sticky taffy.

"They are eccentric characters and I think children, especially, and adults as well, respond very well to eccentric characters. The scene that takes place in the theater is divine really. It's so strange and fantastical that I think that it will really appeal."

"Yes," concurs Saunders. "My favorite moment is when the Other Miss Forcible and the Other Miss Spink zip open their bodies and there are these young, beautiful, thin people leaping out in magnificence."

"They *are* beautiful," confirms Dakota Fanning, who voices Coraline. "In the real world they're old and they've gotten heavier and they're just not in their heyday anymore. But when we are in the Other World, they take off these fat suits and they're these gorgeous, skinny, young actresses. That's what they dream about in the real world, it's what they were a long time ago. They're doing a play, and they just think they're the greatest thing ever. They are having so much fun in this theater with all their Scottie dogs applauding them."

"Miss Spink and Miss Forcible have three Scottish terriers," explains Henry Selick, "and Coraline discovers a whole wall of Scottie dogs with angel wings. When she asks if the dogs are real, the old ladies tell her that they are their sweet departed angels. They couldn't bear to part with them, so they had them stuffed when they died. So the old ladies are a little off their rockers."

Miss Spink gives Coraline a looking stone to help her see the truth.

"It was Henry's idea that the dogs are stuffed," Neil Gaiman points out. "I also love the fact they have knitted angel wings too—that he made the dead dogs angels is somehow really disturbing."

"I especially love the Scottie dogs," says Dawn French. "They've got hundreds of these little dogs who are their audience when they perform, and when the little Scottie dogs pop over to Scottie heaven, they stuff them and they make little sweaters with angel wings on for them."

"At the end of the film," adds Selick, "when the Other World gets dangerous and goes bad, and Coraline sees it for what it really is, the Scottie dogs are turned into bat-dogs. They become bat-winged Scottie dogs, and they come flying out of the sky at Coraline. However, they're really goofy, still. They just can't help it."

"Mr. Bobinsky is the strange upstairs neighbor," explains Henry Selick. "We've turned him into an eight-foot-tall Russian giant. He's very sad. He keeps raw beets in his pockets, because he thinks they're healthy, and he likes to munch on them. He also claims that his famous Jumping Mouse Circus is not ready yet because they are still practicing.

"All the characters who inhabit Coraline's shadowy Other World are surprising and unpredictable, and Mr. Bobinsky has an edge to him that is both comic and villainous."

"Mr. Bobinsky is just very eccentric and sad and lonely in his own way," says Dakota Fanning. "He believes he has this Jumping Mouse Circus, which no one thinks that he really does."

For the voice of the Russian giant, the filmmakers turned to British actor Ian McShane. Although he is probably best known by modern audiences for his Golden Globe Award–winning performance as Al Swearengen on HBO's *Deadwood* (2004–06), McShane's career stretches back to 1962, when he made his film debut in *The Wild and the Willing* (aka *Young and Willing*), about student life during the early 1960s.

He was born in Blackburn, Lancashire, in September 1942. The actor's Scottish-born father, Harry, was a professional football player with Manchester United. McShane studied at the Royal Academy of Dramatic Arts, and various roles in TV series followed throughout the decade, culminating in his performance as Heathcliff in a 1967 BBC production of *Wuthering Heights*.

In the 1980s McShane formed his own production company to make the popular BBC television series *Lovejoy* (1986–94), in which he starred as the eponymous antiques expert who often found himself operating only just on the right side of the law.

"The bad boy is always more fun," states McShane. "It's funny, but when you're in your early twenties, you go ahead and do everything. It's very hard to judge yourself.

"It's like when you're in drama school, and you're playing a sixty-year-old in Russian plays, and you get criticized, and you say, 'What the hell, I'm an eighteen-year-old trying to be a sixty-year-old Russian?'

Tadahiro's character design for Mr. Bobinsky.

"But the bad boy, I had a knack for it from the start."

Although Henry Selick was aware of the actor's body of work, he had not initially considered him for the role of Mr. Bobinsky. "I've known about Ian McShane forever," recalls the director. "He was in this amazing movie called *Sexy Beast* a few years ago. He was a crime boss, and it was a small but super-important part. There was a menace and charm in that character.

"It was just like, wow, I'd forgotten about him. He's great. And then *Deadwood* was happening. He played Al Swearengen, the saloon owner who cuts people's throats. He was a horrible human being, but you really like him."

McShane spent three sessions in a sound studio in Los Angeles recording his voice performance for *Coraline*. "The strange thing about these films is that you don't meet anybody else when you're doing it," reveals the actor. "On the other hand, it can be very interesting, because you're one on one with the director and his vision. You can work together to create something special.

"I really enjoyed working with Henry, who I think is extraordinary. I very much liked *The Nightmare Before Christmas* and *James and the Giant Peach,* which I watched with my grandchildren.

"I really enjoy that kind of animation. With Henry it's strange, spooky, fabulously childlike. Very, very different. He is a very interesting man. And of course, Neil Gaiman is very popular at the moment, and the subject matter was fun."

Selick had heard that McShane could do a good Russian accent, so he turned the character of Mr. Bobinsky into a Russian and then sent the actor a note inviting him to play the role.

LEFT

*M*r. Bobinsky passes along a special message from his dancing mice.

ABOVE

*M*r. Bobinsky greets Coraline.

BELOW

*T*adahiro's character design for the Other Mr. Bobinsky.

other old man

*The Other Mr.
Bobinsky greets
Coraline and the
Other Wybie.*

"I guess he probably saw me on *The West Wing,*" muses McShane, who portrayed a Russian negotiator in a 2002 episode of the hit NBC show. "It was fascinating doing a Russian accent for *Coraline,* and I always enjoy doing accents."

"He wanted to do the part," says Selick. "There's a bottomless well to his voice. He makes Mr. Bobinsky imposing, and scary, and a little cold and aloof. He's a wonderful actor."

LEFT

Ian McShane performs the roles of Mr. Bobinsky and the Other Mr. Bobinsky.

FOLLOWING PAGES

The Other Mr. Bobinsky asks Coraline and the Other Wybie how they liked the show.

"Ian McShane is really funny," confirms Neil Gaiman. "He has this wonderful Russian accent, and he's *blue*—which I will ask Henry to explain one day, and he will. At some point I plan to sidle up to him and say, 'Okay, so tell me about the blue thing . . .'

"What I really have to do is get Henry drunk, and then ask him why Mr. Bobinsky is blue. And then maybe he will tell me."

"Ian McShane also plays the Other Mr. Bobinsky," Selick points out. "He is a much better incarnation—a circus ringmaster introducing the mouse circus and saying Coraline's name correctly. No one says her name right in the real world."

"He has this unbelievable costume," explains Dakota Fanning, "and he's commanding these 'myshkas'—mice—and they're doing these unbelievable acrobatic tricks and playing music. There are mechanical chickens that are actually popping popcorn, and these incredible machines that are making food, and jumping mice spelling out Coraline's name."

"And then there's a final incarnation," adds Selick. "When that Other World's falling apart and Mr. Bobinsky is tottering—you don't know if he's drunk or just about to collapse—Ian McShane made this singsong riddler of a character out of Mr. Bobinsky at the end. It's simply a stellar performance."

"I think that the theme of the film is that things are always better at home," says McShane. "But it is also very spooky and scary. It isn't as gentle as some children's animated films—Henry doesn't pull any punches."

"Our Father, Charlie Jones, is voiced by John Hodgman," Henry Selick explains. "He's the put-upon father. Mother is the leader in the family. They've got a writing assignment they have to finish, and their livelihood depends upon it. His relationship with his wife is a little strained. They're under a lot of pressure."

Born in Brookline, Massachusetts, in June 1971, humorist John Hodgman is probably best known to television viewers as the anthropomorphous PC in the Apple "Get a Mac" advertising campaign.

"He plays the computer that has the virus, who has trouble getting upgraded and so forth," explains Selick. "He has a wonderfully appealing voice."

After graduating from Yale University in 1994, Hodgman worked as a literary agent at Writers House in New York City, where his clients included *Evil Dead* actor Bruce Campbell.

Hodgman is a contributor to *The Paris Review, Wired, McSweeney's Quarterly Concern,* and the *New York Times Magazine* (for which he is editor of the humor section); his first book, published in 2005, was the satirical almanac *The Areas of My Expertise,* which was full of fake facts and absurd stories. The author himself narrated the audiobook version.

"John Hodgman is a writer, first," continues Selick. "He's had a couple of best-selling humor books about his vast knowledge of everything—most of it wrong. He appeared on the *Daily Show,* promoting his book, and I saw him there."

Neil Gaiman first met John Hodgman when he was introduced by him at a reading in New York. "He was my interviewer," recalls Gaiman, "and he said, 'Oh, by the way, I'm in a movie you wrote. I'm going to play the father and the Other Father . . .'"

"He is just wonderful as the father—bemused, very affectionate. He does that thing that fathers do when they embarrass their kids, yet somehow think that they are being cool. But they're not, they are just being really, really embarrassing, and you just want them to go away. He has that down perfectly, and you both love him for it and wish he would stop. I think any actor who can give that performance is doing an incredible job."

"The father is a little warmer with Coraline," explains Henry Selick. "The mother is under pressure and has a tougher time being a nurturing mother to Coraline. Father tries a little harder to be there for her. He cracks bad jokes. He has a song he's made up that he's sung to Coraline her whole life. He calls her his 'twitchy witchy girl.'

"I was listening to a lot of father voices, and John's voice just sounded so perfect against Dakota Fanning and Teri Hatcher. We had those two confirmed at that point. He is a hell of a writer, so he added some improvisation. As did Teri Hatcher, who is incredible at improvising. She also added a lot of great lines.

The Other Father greets Coraline.

CORALINE'S OTHER FATHER

ABOVE AND OPPOSITE

*T*adahiro's character designs for the Other Father.

TOP RIGHT

*T*adahiro's concept design for the Other Father's Praying Mantis Tractor.

RIGHT

*T*adahiro's concept design for the Other Father's piano that "plays him."

"John brings this hesitant, stuttering approach to this father who is smart but who can't multitask. He can only do one thing at a time. He types with single fingers. He's not real talented. But he's the person who cooks the meals and he puts everything into it. They're horrible meals—he's a terrible cook. But he does it with love."

"The real father is consumed in his garden catalog," explains Dakota Fanning. "He's very ragged and tired. His face is so long and sad, as if there's no hope."

In the Other World, the Other Father is the antithesis of Coraline's real father and can sing perfectly.

"He's a smooth guy," says Selick. "It's what Coraline thinks she'd want her real father to be like. You always try to come up with something clear and simple, so for John Hodgman playing the Other Father, the original direction was, 'Just be Dean Martin.'

"Because I knew he could never be Dean Martin, John is a lot of fun. He also has to sing really well. But when he was doing his Dean Martin impression, it was more like Bing Crosby. So it's this crazy thing that really works well.

"The Other Father is smooth. He's fun. He makes little jokes. He plays the piano and writes songs for Coraline instead of typing away."

"The Other Father is just consumed with making up songs for his daughter Coraline," Fanning reveals. "He has no control in his relationship. He's just a robot being controlled by the Other Mother. He really doesn't want to be hurting Coraline, but the Other Mother is making him."

FOLLOWING PAGES

The Other Father listens to Coraline's giggles from his Praying Mantis Tractor.

While in the Other World, Coraline also encounters the same black cat that she inadvertently insulted in the real world. This enigmatic feline has the ability to move between the two worlds by crawling through a magical Cat Way Tree.

"It's an amazing cat," says Henry Selick. "He's Coraline's reluctant guardian angel. It's Wybie's cat, and he claims that it is wild, feral, but it hates to get its feet wet.

"In the Other World, Coraline thinks it is the Other Cat, like everything else. But it doesn't have buttons for eyes, like her Other Mother and Father or the Other Wybie and Other Mr. Bobinsky do.

"In fact, it's the same cat, and it can speak in the Other World. It can travel in and out at will because there are cat ways in and out of most any place."

The voice of the Cat is supplied by Emmy Award–winning stage and screen actor Keith David. Born in New York City's Harlem in June 1956, David realized that he wanted to become an actor after playing the Cowardly Lion in a school production of *The Wizard of Oz*. He subsequently enrolled in Manhattan's School of the Performing Arts. Later, he graduated from Juilliard, and during the early 1980s honed his craft touring with John Houseman's Acting Company in productions of William Shakespeare's *A Midsummer Night's Dream* and Samuel Beckett's *Waiting for Godot*.

Thanks to his deep, compelling voice, he is also a popular contributor to various cartoon series.

The Cat greets Coraline in the Other World.

ABOVE

The Cat wakes Coraline up.

RIGHT

Keith David performs the role of the Cat that helps Coraline find her way through the Other World.

Wybie's cat turns out to be very brave and wise, as Dakota Fanning explains: "The Cat just thinks he's the greatest thing—he thinks he's the cat's meow! He ends up helping Coraline in her plan to escape from the Other World."

However, being a cat, he cannot help but play with his prey a little bit when he catches a cute Kangaroo Mouse in his paws.

"Of course, the jumping mouse turns out to be a spy in disguise," reveals Henry Selick. "It's actually a black, creepy rat. The Other Mother's spies are rats, and they are disguised as cute jumping mice.

"The rats themselves are, I think, a lot of fun. They're not the rats of *Flushed Away* or *Ratatouille*. They're not cute, lovable rats. These are awful, creepy little rats."

ABOVE

The Cat gives Coraline a "look," then departs.

FOLLOWING PAGES

Coraline and the Cat try to escape the Other World and end up at the Other House.

While adapting Neil Gaiman's original book for the screen, Henry Selick added a main character of his own: "Wybie Lovat is a character that I invented for the movie," explains the director. "He didn't exist in the book, and of course, you are always worried about the fans of the book complaining, 'Why did you stick this kid in there?'

"But Coraline has a lot of internal thoughts, and the only friend she has is the cat, who is in the real world and, of course, can't talk. I needed somebody for her to share her thoughts with, and create a little more conflict.

"So Wybie Lovat is basically this neighborhood kid who is very clever, but very much an outsider. He knows a lot, but may or may not be connected with some bad magic. Wybie's built himself an electric bicycle that he uses to patrol the woods. He's also befriended the cat, who turns out to be a very important character in the movie—pretty much Coraline's guardian angel.

"In fact, Wybie's grandmother owns the house that Coraline and her family have just moved into. They are renting one of the main floors, and there are some dark secrets in that house. Wybie has a few clues about those secrets, but he doesn't really know. He's quirky and lonely. He probably doesn't have many friends."

"Yes, Henry made up one character, which is Wybie," confirms Neil Gaiman. "Everybody else is solidly from the book. But he created Wybie because there are places in the book where Coraline needs somebody to talk to. In the book you can have what she's thinking, which is fine. However, in a film it's so much better to give her somebody to converse with."

"I thought Coraline's friend Wybie was a really good addition," agrees Gaiman's youngest daughter, Maddy, "because in the book it seems like when Coraline doesn't have anyone there for her, she turns to the Cat. But in the movie she can turn to Wybie, because he's there for her."

Tadahiro's character designs for Wybie Lovat.

ABOVE

*Wybie and the
Cat greet Coraline
in the fog.*

LEFT

*Coraline's
annoying
neighbor Wybie
Lovat.*

The Characters   189

"When she moves into the new house, she doesn't really like him at first, but it's just nice that she has a friend there. I like that."

Wybie (short for Wyborne) Lovat is voiced by Robert Bailey Jr., who, since the mid-1990s, has guest-starred on numerous TV shows as well as movies *Mission to Mars* (2000), *Baby Bedlam* (2000), *Dragonfly* (2002), and *The Happening* (2008).

"Wybie is a bit strange," Dakota Fanning reveals. "Wybie is the first person that Coraline meets, and she just thinks he's weird. He gives her this doll that looks like her and, after this doll comes into her life, she discovers the Other World. So it's linked to the doll in some way.

"At the end of the story, Wybie is frantic to get the doll back, because he realizes that he made a mistake, and that his grandmother needs it. In the Other World, he really helps Coraline a lot, and when she comes back into the real world they learn to be friends."

"In the end," adds Selick, "Wybie is someone who has to be convinced that Coraline's not lying about this wild Other World and the dangers that it poses. He eventually comes around, and is a very true friend to her."

TOP LEFT

Coraline reads Wybie's note.

ABOVE LEFT

A Coraline doll.

ABOVE

The actual size of a Coraline doll is evident here, in the hands of a LAIKA animator.

LEFT

Tadahiro's character design for the Other Wybie.

ABOVE

*C*oraline
unstitches the
Other Wybie's
painfully huge
grin.

RIGHT

*W*ybie tells
Coraline that he
believes her.

The three button-eyed ghost children are voiced by Hannah Kaiser, Aankha Neal, and George Selick.

"They've been locked away in a closet-prison by the Other Mother," explains Henry Selick. "She basically lures children to the Other World with treasures and treats, and then tells them she loves them and feeds on their life-force. And once she's done, she throws them away in the closet."

By their archaic manner of speech and references to their former lives, Coraline realizes that the ghost children have been locked away for a very long time.

"These are sad children," says Selick. "One is from pioneer times, and another is from the turn of the last century. One of them is Wybie's great-aunt, who disappeared as a child."

Tadahiro's character designs for the three ghost children.

From Director Henry Selick and Author Neil Gaiman

Coraline

Some

doors

should

never

be

opened.

In Theatres 2008

4

The Other Coralines

We have eyes and we have nerveses.
We have tails we have teeth.
You'll all get what you deserveses.
When we rise from underneath.

Since it was first published in 2002, Neil Gaiman's *Coraline* has become a cultural phenomenon around the world.

Not only has the multiple award–winning novel been translated into more than thirty languages, but it has also been adapted into diverse and various media that transcend the printed word.

"One of the strangest things about my career," reveals Gaiman, "is that I've been blessed by the gods of good timing. Projects seem to come out at exactly the right time, or come out together."

Originally produced for a competition in 2004, a two-minute short film of *Coraline* was created by Italian design students Dario Spinelli, Gabriele Rossi, and Federico Mattioli using a combination of live-action and cut-out animation to encapsulate the story of Neil Gaiman's novel.

OPPOSITE

Conceptual poster idea for the film.

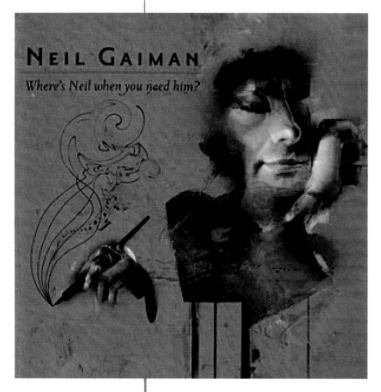

"It started out as a university project," reveals Spinelli, "and was meant as a film trailer for the novel. It was intended to convey the atmosphere of the book and to attract the curiosity of the viewer (and future reader, hopefully).

"It uses a mixed technique: the real world is live-action, while the 'Other' house is an animated pop-up book, with paper-doll characters (the Cat being the exception).

"The idea was to render clearly the difference between the two worlds, while maintaining the particular atmosphere of the novel."

"It's beautiful," says Gaiman.

The Italian inter-titles translate as "We've been waiting for you," "Who are you?" and "I'm your Other Mother," while the accompanying music is from Piano Concerto No. 3 by Rachmaninoff, played on a celesta.

The CD art for **Where's Neil When You Need Him?**

The film was posted online by BonsaiNinja Studio in 2006. "It was made before the official film was announced," Dario Spinelli explains. "We put so much effort into it that we thought it was a pity not to show it to somebody else."

Released in July that same year on the Philadelphia-based independent label Dancing Ferret Discs, the compilation album *Where's Neil When You Need Him?* is a tribute CD to Neil Gaiman and his work.

Conceived by label owner Patrick Rodgers, who also acted as music supervisor, the album contains seventeen tracks by various artists inspired by the author's fiction and characters. Among the acts that contributed to the project were Gaiman's longtime friend Tori Amos (whose song "Space Dog" provided the album's title) and Goth/metal band Tapping the Vein.

Two of the tracks, recorded by Brooklyn cello-rock band Rasputina and British singer Rose Berlin, the teenage daughter of Dean Garcia from the 1990s music group Curve, were directly inspired by *Coraline*.

Dave McKean created original artwork for the CD, while Gaiman himself contributed the extensive liner notes. Gerard Way, the lead singer with New York alternative band My Chemical Romance, wrote the introduction to the album booklet.

Also in 2006, Irish theatrical puppet troupe Púca Puppets developed *Coraline* for the stage as a coproduction with the Éigse Carlow Arts Festival. Specializing in theater with puppets for both adults and children, the company utilized a unique form of puppet-theater known as "Czech-Black." This involves the puppeteers dressing from head to toe in black and manipulating their puppets via attached rods against a black backdrop. Coupled with atmospheric lighting and music and sound effects, when the puppet is framed in a carefully focused beam of light, the puppeteer becomes "invisible" and the puppets appear to move around of their own volition.

As part of two years of intensive script and design development, the production carried out research and consultation with children and child psychologists, thanks to an Arts Council bursary and a Dublin City Council Award.

ABOVE

Ireland's Púca Puppets developed a stage version of **Coraline** *in 2006.*

LEFT

Púca Puppets stage a scene where Coraline meets the three ghost children.

Directed by movement specialist and former actress Sue Mythen, with lighting by Moyra D'Arcy, and original sound and music composed by Slavek Kwi, the presentation utilized more than fifteen oversized puppets, a raised rotating stage, and a number of set pieces in collaboration with artist Fiona Dowling. The cast consisted of Margot Jones, Joe Moylan, and Niamh Lawlor as Coraline.

"It looked absolutely terrifying, and beautiful, and very, very faithful," observed Neil Gaiman.

Púca staged the seventy-five-minute show on June 2 at the 2006 World Puppet Art Festival in Prague, Czech Republic, with support from Culture Ireland.

Following a two-week run at the Projects Arts Centre in Dublin, *Coraline* then went on tour around Ireland in October and November of that same year.

"Alice with attitude in a dark Wonderland," was how the *Times Educational Supplement* described it. "A gripping and moving tale which restores child readers to a safe reality."

"*Coraline* may have been written with children in mind, but it's an occasionally chilling and atmospheric fable that will appeal to young and old alike," was how Daragh Reddin reviewed it in *Metro,* while Michael Moffatt concurred in the *Irish Mail on Sunday*: "This is a brave production in the era of computer

effects and electronic wizardry, but it shows the power of a well-told, witty story to engage the emotions and fire the imagination."

In March 2007, Swedish children's and youth theater group Mittiprickteatern premiered a stage production of *Coraline* at the Theatre Påfågeln in Stockholm, prior to touring the country.

Dramatized by director Cleo Boman, the hour-long production featured Ulrika Hansson as Coraline, Eva Welinder as the Other Mother, and Magnus Munkesjö as the Other Father. Other roles were taken by

Lennart Gustafsson, with Henrik Gustafsson replacing David Nordström for the show's fall 2007 and 2008 revivals.

"Cleo Boman has created a fantastic performance in every sense of the word," declared reviewer Catarina Nitz in *Pavee Kuriren*. "Eva Welinder is wonderfully frightening as the Other Mother, and fun as the telesales mother . . . Personally, I was elated."

The show was mounted with support from the National Kulturråd, Stockholm Council, and the Culture Stockholm.

Another theatrical adaptation of *Coraline,* directed by Leigh Silverman, with music and lyrics by Stephin Merritt and book by David Greenspan, is set to have its world premiere at the Lucille Lortel Theatre in New York in the summer of 2009.

"That came about because Stephin Merritt loves *Coraline,*" explains Neil Gaiman.

"For me Neil's genius, like that of early Bugs Bunny, is in the asides," observes Merritt. "The story may be playing fast and loose with archetypes, but it's the giggling throughout that makes you stick around to cry at the end."

Although much of the show is underscored, as the composer explains, "Some of the vocal sections are only a few lines long. I think there are about thirty songs, but one is fifteen minutes long and has very sung text."

"I've heard most of the songs, sung by Stephin himself," reveals Gaiman, "and they're wonderful. It's also very, very faithful to the book, which makes me happy."

"We have ridden a pendulum back and forth between wanting to show everything—trees gradually blurring, house flattening, pullover made of stars, man made of rats—and wanting to tell the story entirely verbally, down to actually reading the stage directions aloud," Merritt confirms. "The story hasn't changed much, but it inevitably will."

Iconoclastic singer-songwriter Stephin Merritt has released a number of albums under such band names as The 6ths, The Gothic Archies, and Future Bible Heroes. With his synth-pop band The Magnetic Fields, he has produced, written, and recorded nine albums between 1991 and 2008.

The Magnetic Fields' 1999 triple-album *69 Love Songs* featured children's author Daniel Handler (aka Lemony Snicket) playing accordion,

Scenes from Mittiprickteatern's **Coraline,** *with Magnus Munkesjö as the Other Father, Ulrika Hansson as Coraline, and Eva Welinder as the Other Mother.*

and Merritt used the name The Baudelaire Memorial Orchestra for a song written for *Lemony Snicket's A Series of Unfortunate Events* (2004), while he also recorded music for the audiobook versions of the series under The Gothic Archies attribution.

"Stephin had done songs for each of the *Lemony Snicket* audiobooks," explains Gaiman, "and I asked him to compose some songs for the *Coraline* audiobook, also done by HarperCollins. He wrote a song called 'You Are Not My Mother and I Want to Go Home,' and the rat songs are the creepiest things you've ever heard.

"He sang one to me while we were crossing a street in New York, and a woman stopped dead in her tracks, terrified, and nearly got hit by a car!"

Merritt, a former editor of *Spin* magazine and *Time Out New York,* who has also composed music for the theater, films, and television, has been developing a stage musical based around Gaiman's novel since 2005.

"Stuck in my head for years has been the following over-the-top theme song," he reveals, "which we are not even using. Sing this like Nico:

> *Which beast will leap*
> *on sleep—*
> *ing Coraline?*
>
> *Which fate befall*
> *our small,*
> *sweet Coraline?*
>
> *Who will warn her?*
> *Who will WARN HER?*

"Stephin had wanted to do a *Coraline* musical, but I had to tell him no, because the rights were all tied up," explains Gaiman. "Then we got the rights back, so I called him and told him that if he still wanted to do it, he could."

Obie Award–winning actor, writer, and director David Greenspan, who wrote the book for the musical *Coraline,* is also set to play the seductive Other Mother in the stage production. Since he began writing in 1986, Greenspan has had around twenty plays produced Off-Broadway, most notably at the Contemporary Theatre

The Cat shows Coraline the mother/father doll.

and Art in SoHo. His credits include such theatrical farces as *Dead Mother, or Shirley Not in Vain* and *She Stoops to Comedy* (in which he portrayed a woman playing a man).

Tony Kushner, the Pulitzer Prize–winning author of *Angels in America* and other plays, has described Greenspan as "Probably all-round the most talented theater artist of my generation."

"Being a theater professional who goes to the movies almost every day, and the theater a few times a month, I can tell you there is almost no overlap between the two audiences," observes Stephin Merritt. "I don't know why.

"Like the graphic- and straight-novel audiences—most of the people I know read a lot, but only in one medium. If Neil is the first writer to cross over from one to the other and keep his readers, then that could be because his way with an archetype goes deeper than mere medium and genre.

"We do hope to piggyback on the success of the novel, but I hold out no hope that a stop-action animated film of *Coraline,* however gorgeous and popular, will send its audience to see an Off-Broadway musical. If somehow it does, then Danny Elfman will soon be doing *The Nightmare Before Christmas* at the Winter Garden."

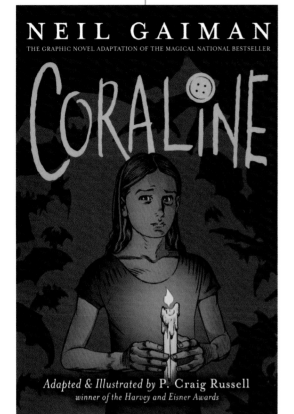

"At the point where graphic novels started becoming huge in America," Neil Gaiman recalls, "HarperCollins approached me and said they would like to do a *Coraline* graphic novel. And I said we should talk to Craig Russell."

The multiple Harvey Award and Eisner Award–winning P. [Philip] Craig Russell had previously collaborated with Neil Gaiman on a number of comics projects, including the critically acclaimed "Ramadan" sequence in *Sandman* #50, published by DC Comics/Vertigo in 1993, and the first story, "Death and Venice," in the 2003 Sandman collection *Endless Night*. Russell also adapted the author's short story "Murder Mysteries" into comics format for Dark Horse Books in 2002, and he is currently working on a comics version of the author's 1999 stand-alone volume *Sandman: The Dream Hunters*.

Russell admits that what attracted him to adapting another Neil Gaiman project was the author himself: "His stories are immediately engaging," he says, "and even at their creepiest are always witty and beautifully written."

"The novel *Coraline* was even more so, as its worldview was filtered through the eyes of its young protagonist. Coraline is a self-reliant, curious, and adventurous little girl ready to face her fears. She's a great role model for kids—feisty and loving, without ever being sticky about it. I liked her."

"Craig is the only person that I trust completely to adapt my stuff," reveals Gaiman, "because he's not just an immensely brilliant artist—which he is—but he's really good at taking something in the book and knowing how many pages that will fill."

Although the graphic version is very faithful to the original book, by necessity Russell had to trim scenes from the thirty-thousand-word novel to fit the number of pages he had to work with.

"That's always difficult," he admits. "The trick is to take the entire novel apart and then to put it back together in such a way that the reader has no idea that anything has been left out."

However, there was one unexpected complication. As an artist, Russell usually uses real people to pose for most of his characters. The little girl he was using as the model for Coraline was in virtually every frame of the graphic novel. As there was no way for the artist to get all the photo references he needed in a single session, they would get together every couple of months when the girl's busy school schedule permitted.

"After about a year, I noticed that she was growing taller and soon would not be so little any longer," recalls Russell. "I've had models get fat on me, but I've never had one 'grow up' on me."

OPPOSITE TOP

*T*he cover of the graphic novel edition of *Coraline*, adapted and illustrated by P. Craig Russell.

OPPOSITE BOTTOM AND ABOVE

*S*ome of P. Craig Russell's original art pages from the graphic novel of **Coraline**.

It took Russell almost two years to produce the 186 pages for his graphic adaptation of *Coraline*. "I always start by simultaneously writing the script and designing the layouts," he explains. "Sometimes a visual solution to a scene occurs to me first and I fashion the script to fit it. Sometimes it's all script first and then I try to find the pictures that most effectively illustrate it."

One significant change that Russell made in his version was the design of the Other Father at the point where he has degenerated into a pale and swollen grub-like creature banished to the cellar by the Other Mother.

"In the novel he chases Coraline around the cellar," Russell explains. "That works in the writing, but I found that for the character to perform the actions, he still needed more human-like characteristics in order to move.

"So my design solution was to have the face and skin in an advanced state of decomposition, while being human enough to move quickly."

"There's stuff in there that is scary," observes Neil Gaiman. "It's actually quite disturbing."

HarperCollins published the hardcover graphic novel of *Coraline* in June 2008. Adapted and illustrated by P. Craig Russell, it is lettered by Todd Klein, also known for his award-winning work on *Sandman*.

Russell confirms that he is looking forward to seeing Henry Selick's movie version of the book: "As always, when seeing another artist's—or, in the case of animation, many other artists'—solutions to the same material, I'm left thinking, 'Now why didn't I think of that?' From the trailer to the movie, I can see a completely different visual approach than mine, and one that looks quite successfully creepy."

At the Cannes Film Festival in May 2006, it was announced that Focus Features would handle worldwide distribution of the film version of *Coraline*.

Part of NBC Universal, one of the world's leading media and entertainment companies, Focus Features is a motion picture production, financing, and worldwide distribution company committed to bringing moviegoers the most original stories from the world's most innovative filmmakers.

Meanwhile, to accommodate its expanded production slate, LAIKA began construction on a new animation campus on thirty acres of land in Tualatin, Oregon, twelve miles south of Portland.

Comprising four buildings designed by TVA Architects, Inc., who also designed the award-winning Nike World Campus in Beaverton, Oregon, the world-class animation and film production facility is due to be completed in 2010.

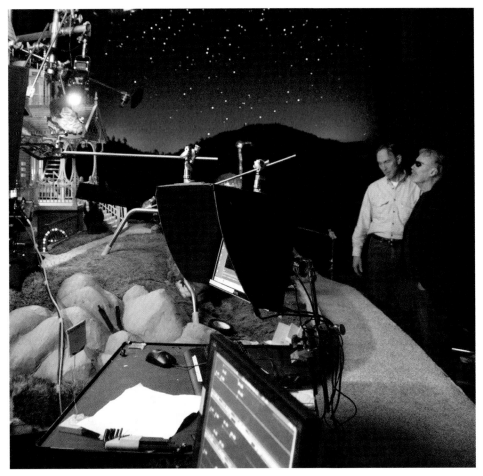

"We want to have a really broad range of projects," explains Travis Knight, the studio's vice-president of animation, "and I guess the thing that ultimately unites them all is a singular, really creative voice.

"With *Coraline* you already have this fantastic story that's really interesting, and weird, and dark, and funny. So it's incredible source material. But behind all that is Henry Selick, driving the film. He brought this whole different side and this whole different life to it.

"But then, of course, filmmaking is a collaborative effort. So it's a matter of working with everybody that we have at LAIKA—scores of people and puppets, and story and design, and editing and animation, lighting and camera. All these people bring something of themselves to these really unique projects."

"I've lived with *Coraline* for more than five years," says Selick, "from when I first read the galleys of the book before it was published, through convincing Bill Mechanic to be the first producer and pay me to write it. Then having my first draft utterly rejected, and stewing on that for a few months before going back to work. So I've lived with the project for a long time.

TOP

*A*n exterior set
with rain machine
and background.

LEFT

*P*re-vision artist
Morgan Hay tests
out possible ideas
for the Other
World destruction
sequence.

The Other Coralines   209

"I know it intimately. So I gathered some of the best people in the world. I had an incredible crew, many of them going back more than twenty years.

"It was incredibly exciting to see *Coraline* coming to life before me. Although I know the story very well, it was nice to see what other people brought to the project. They got in tune with the vision and then they expanded it. People such as Pete Kozachik, the director of photography; Chris Butler, head of story; Bo Henry, in charge of set construction, and art directors Philip Brotherton and Tom Proost, who worked with him. It was so great to see this family of filmmakers come together and focus on the movie."

"Every time I've worked on a stop-motion project," reveals head story-artist Chris Butler, "it pushes the technique so much further—to the point where, sometimes, you can't believe that they're puppets. With *Coraline* we were working on computer screens instead of paper. So there were a lot of things that are innovative that come out of the need to make this movie better, to really put us on the map.

"I love that this movie is going to be something different. I think that it is going to be something that will be really special, and that is worth all the hard work."

"I'm particularly interested in finding ways to do really avant-garde animation," agrees lead animator Travis Knight. "Animation that is really unique and really pushes the sense of what people think animation can and should be.

"But behind everything, I think here at LAIKA we have to put our own spin on it. We have to find our own way to tell a story, and there are only so many stories you can tell."

Coraline completed its eighteen-month shooting schedule in November 2008. As director Henry Selick sums up the film: "It's the story of a not-happy-enough girl, smart and brave but very bored, who discovers a better version of her life through a secret door in the old house she and her parents have just moved into.

"She meets her Other Mother and Other Father—improved versions of the real ones, except they have black button eyes. This other version of her life seems like a child's paradise with great food, magical shows, living gardens, etc. But there's a big price to pay if Coraline wants to stay there.

"Her parents are too busy for her, so she's just very lonely. Then, when she crosses over into this Other World, she realizes that maybe she doesn't want to get everything that she wants, and that the grass is not always greener on the other side.

"What it shows about kids and their relationships with their parents is that they just want some time and attention. They just want to be loved, and for parents to play with them. To get the most out of the time that they share together. What all kids really want of their parents is time and love.

"In Coraline's life, she's not really getting that because her parents are trying to adjust to this new place and working hard, and she doesn't feel like it will ever be

the same. So when she is captured by the Other Mother, she appreciates what she had and would give anything to get that back."

"In certain circumstances, I think real-life relationships between kids and parents can be difficult," agrees Teri Hatcher, who is the voice of both Coraline's mother and the frightening Other Mother. "We all have different things to deal with, and I think our children will always demand as much as they can get from us.

"Sometimes we can give it to them, and sometimes we can't. In my relationship with my daughter, I've always tried to believe in really just communicating honestly. Instead of letting the resentment build up, being able to say, 'I'm having a really hard day—I'd be able to do this for you another day, but today I just can't.' I think we have done that consistently throughout her upbringing, and I feel that my daughter and I have a great relationship.

"I think the movie speaks about communication between parents and children, and how maybe that needs to be looked at before things go awry. But, not to be too serious about it, ultimately it's an entertaining, scary story."

"I do think that the worst thing a child can imagine is losing their parents," says Dawn French, who voices both versions of Miss Forcible. "That is what happens in this film, although it appears the opposite happens because extra parents turn up."

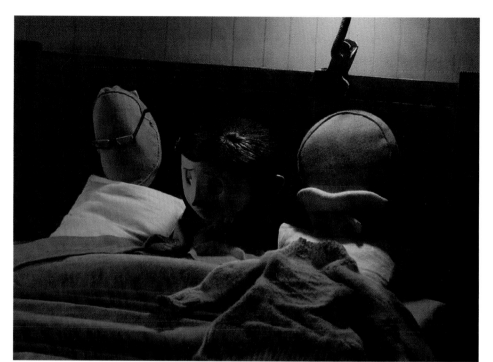

In the end, Coraline's parents are back home.

"But that is also a child's fantasy," points out Jennifer Saunders, the voice of Miss Spink and her Other World alter ego. "That you somehow lose your real parents, but you get adopted by some really nice people and you can play out that fantasy. But the reality is that it's awful."

"In this film," continues Dawn French, "you know that Coraline's mother hasn't got time to cook—she's busy—and the father used to make up songs, but he's also busy. So when she meets the Other Parents, who've got lovely twinkly button eyes, they do all the things that Coraline really wishes her real parents would do.

"But then the horrible day comes when the most unthinkable thing is suggested. Coraline's Other Mother proposes that her eyes are replaced by buttons, and she has the needle-and-thread and the buttons ready to do it! To me, you can't get any darker than that really!"

"I don't think that anyone is perfect," says Dakota Fanning. "I don't think anyone does everything right. But I think that everyone should just be patient with what-ever they have. Everything happens for a reason. You just need to make the best of it, and realize that sometimes you don't want what you wish for. Sometimes, you should just accept what you have, because that's really the best thing for you."

RIGHT

Coraline's father jokes around with her before bed.

OPPOSITE TOP

Coraline discovers the broken snow globe after escaping from the Other Mother.

OPPOSITE BOTTOM

Coraline's mother drives her home in the family's VW.

As far back as 2005, New York indie band They Might Be Giants were rumored to be writing and recording a number of songs for *Coraline.*

Formed in 1982 by John Flansburgh and John Linnell, and taking their name from the 1971 movie starring George C. Scott and Joanne Woodward, the lineup of the unconventional alternative-rock band currently includes Marty Beller, Dan Miller, and Danny Weinkauf. Best known on both sides of the Atlantic for their 1990 hit "Birdhouse in Your Soul," the group has sold more than four million albums worldwide.

They have also recorded theme songs for a number of television shows, including Comedy Central's *The Daily Show,* Adult Swim's *The Oblongs,* the Disney Channel's *Mickey Mouse Clubhouse* and *Higglytown Heroes,* and Fox Television Network's *Malcolm in the Middle,* which earned them a Grammy Award in 2002.

"They've done a lot of work for TV themes," confirms Henry Selick. "I first met with them in 1996, and then I hooked up with them again.

"Early on, we considered making *Coraline* a musical, and they did some beautiful, astonishing demo songs. Over time, the musical idea faded, and we have ended up using just one of their most excellent songs, which the Other Father sings to Coraline."

Oscar-nominated French composer Bruno Coulais supplied the final musical score for *Coraline*. Initially trained as a composer of contemporary classical music, he moved into film music in the late 1980s, scoring such popular movies as *The Crimson Rivers* (*Les rivières pourpres*) and *Belphégor, le fantôme du Louvre*.

"Bruno Coulais just happened to be one of the numerous CDs that we listened to to try and find something that was an honest portrayal of the magic of childhood, but which also had the terror of childhood," reveals Henry Selick. "It was just this fit. Most of what he sent was perfect from day one. It's a very, very fine line, because the tone of this movie is always on a razor's edge. We wanted it to be fun in the right moments, but also to have life-and-death consequences in others."

In June 2008, leading interactive entertainment publisher and software company D3Publisher, a subsidiary of D3, Inc., announced an agreement with the Universal Pictures Digital Platforms Group to produce a series of video games based around the film.

"The video game plays up on Coraline's character as an explorer, and as a collector of things—as someone very adventurous and curious—and juxtaposes the two worlds as we do in the film. There are also a lot of really scary elements that the video game can amplify," said Henry Selick.

"The alternative reality–based plot of *Coraline* translates exceptionally well to an interactive gaming adventure," confirms Yoji Takenaka, executive vice-president and chief operating officer of D3P in North America and Europe. "We enjoyed working closely with the filmmakers and the team at Universal and Focus Features to authentically portray the film's unique cast of characters and allow players of all ages to experience not only key environments and moments from the movie, but also elements that go beyond the feature film."

Henry Selick agrees that there are many elements of the film that can definitely be expanded upon in the video-game versions: "What Coraline has to do is find the lost eyes of the ghost children," he explains. "She has to discover where her parents

Other Mother creates a thunderstorm and a "Welcome Home" cake to entertain and entice Coraline.

are hidden after they have been kidnapped by the Other Mother. There are entire universes to explore, to look for these hidden elements.

"She discovers she has a magic viewing stone with a hole in it, given to her by the two old ladies downstairs. It turns out to be a very important weapon against evil. Looking through that stone, Coraline can hunt for the ghost children's eyes, her parents, and anything else we want to put in there.

"So there's the garden, which basically can go on and on. There's a dark, dangerous well out in the woods, which is something Coraline is first warned about in the very beginning of the story. So that's a place to explore, and so forth."

"*Coraline* is a fantastically imagined world, filled with quirky characters and unexpected events," explains Bill Kispert, vice-president and general manager, interactive, at Universal Pictures Digital Platforms Group. "With just the right blend of humor, adventure, and spookiness, it is the perfect source material for a truly unique game."

With console products developed by Papaya Studios and the handheld systems produced in Q1 2009 by ART, *Coraline (The Game)* is a surrealistic adventure aimed at gamers of all ages, launched to coincide with the North American release of the movie by Focus Features in February 2009.

Among other tie-in marketing campaigns being rolled out around the same time, there are in-store promotions for *Coraline* with Macy's and the fast-food chain Carl's Jr. in the United States and Mexico. Hallmark is selling cards and gift-wrap based around the movie, while a *Coraline* doll has been created by NECA for sale through Hot Topic and similar outlets.

"It's rare to see a movie that you can watch again and again and again, and feel like you will never know every detail of it," enthuses Dakota Fanning, who admits that she does not want to give too much of the film's plot away. "So I don't want to go into detail, like about the chickens that are popping popcorn in the Jumping Mouse Circus, and the milkshake chandeliers. But I will say it's just a wonderful fantasy that you're not going to want to leave.

"But you will also learn something from it, and have a good time watching it. Parents will also enjoy watching it, and I think their children will appreciate them more after seeing it."

"As a mom," says Teri Hatcher, "I am always complaining that when you go to the Cineplex, there are sixteen movie theaters and fourteen of them are rated 'R' and the other two are 'PG-13.' It's just hard to find good-quality, entertaining movies for the family, and that's what *Coraline* is."

"*Coraline* is not just for girls," Henry Selick points out. "The boys are going to love her, because the movie will be scary and spooky and filled with creepy-crawly things. Rats that are spies, and bugs that are chocolates, and snakes and snails and puppy-dog tails. So it's really a film for both boys and girls."

"Yes, definitely," agrees Dakota Fanning, "and it's a cool movie to go see because it is such new technology that they're using for this. Like I said, *The Wizard of Oz* and *Alice in Wonderland* are two of the greatest family films, but they're also very dark and scary. *Coraline* also has very scary and frightening elements, but because it's in 3-D, with the models and that interesting look, I think that it will only be scary up to a certain point. But then you'll see something else that will intrigue you—the popcorn is going to be flying at you from the chicken poppers!

"I think it is a movie that everyone can watch over and over and over again," adds the young actress, "which is something that I love to do."

"I just think the animation is so terrific," says Teri Hatcher. "The mastery of the puppeteering—the handmade models, the clothes are all hand-sewn—it is an unbelievable level of artistic genius. All these craftsmen who can create these puppets and move them tiny bit by tiny bit. It's just magnificent how it's all shot. It makes me even more proud to be in the movie.

"I think we're at a stage where getting to see *Coraline* in really good quality 3-D, which is what this is, will be an amazing experience for people. It is just not like the 3-D I grew up with. It's so amazing and real, and really scary—because of the things that come out of the screen at you. It's just beautiful.

"I think people are going to love it. It's a really great story, and it's told in an original way."

"I hope audiences will get their bucket of popcorn and value for money," says Dawn French, "and frankly, I think they will have that with this film. I think it is genuinely a film that the whole family can go to because it works on all sorts of levels.

"There is a solid, properly frightening story for children, and there is also a level on which adults can connect with it as well. Sometimes it is difficult to take youngsters to animation when it's only for them, but that's not the case with this film. In fact, it's quite British in that way."

"I think that audiences will enjoy *Coraline* enormously," adds Ian McShane. "It's very different."

"It is so exciting to be a part of this whole experience with Teri Hatcher, and John Hodgman, and Henry Selick, and getting to collaborate with such a brilliant director," says Dakota Fanning. "I don't think I can ever do what he does—moving the mouths, replacing the heads, putting the clothes on. If I was on the set and had to do Henry's job I think I would just cry!

"But I'll have this forever to show my children. This whole experience has been really amazing. I'll always remember it, and I'm so proud to be a part of it."

"It's fun to be involved in something that you're really proud of," agrees Teri Hatcher. "It's been the best experience. I really feel proud of it, and it's been a great journey."

"I think the technical process, which I was very aware of, having just walked around the sets and puppet workshops, is breathtaking," reveals the original book's illustrator, Dave McKean. "Certainly the animation and 3-D photography is really beautiful, and the design by the Japanese illustrator Tadahiro is wonderful and has a real abstract expressionism to it. I don't think anyone will have any doubt about the love, care, and attention to detail that has gone into the making of the film."

"I think Henry Selick is an incredible example of a filmmaker who really has a unique point of view," says LAIKA's vice president of animation Travis Knight, "and every film that we make has to have that special quality of the filmmaker behind it. Someone who really has a powerful vision and voice. We are in this second golden age of animation, and LAIKA is at the forefront of that resurgence."

"What I love about *Coraline*," says Neil Gaiman, "is that I didn't get the feeling that anybody involved in making it was thinking about the grosses on the day of release. Everybody was just concerned about making a good film.

"No matter how well it does when it comes out, the important question is how will *Coraline* sell on DVD? In fifteen years time, how many people will have actually seen it? And twenty years from now, how many people who saw it when they were children are going to be buying it for their kids?

"That has always been what is interesting and important for me. As a writer—even as a number one *New York Times* bestselling author—I am always very aware that I'm not writing the book for that initial spurt of publicity and attention. I'm writing a book for thirty years from now.

"We recently celebrated the twentieth anniversary of *Sandman*. And just the idea that there are people reading it now who were not even conceived when the first issue came out is really cool. That is part of what I've always tried to do.

"It seems to me that that is what Henry has tried to do with *Coraline*. There was no point at which I lost faith in Henry. LAIKA has not necessarily made a film that lasts

just for the moment. They are making something that lasts forever. That's what Walt Disney did, and I think that it is important and I am proud of them for that."

"Neil Gaiman, the author of the book *Coraline,* has an incredibly wide range of audience," confirms Henry Selick. "I think that like *Harry Potter,* there are a lot of adults who love the book just as much as the children do. The *Coraline* movie is going to appeal to those adults as well. It's smart, scary, and visually very inventive."

"I think that the look of the movie is a very, very strange combination of very contemporary and very classic," Gaiman reveals. "It has a 1950s look that reminds me somewhat of children's illustrations of that period. They have taken a look from about fifty years ago, and then put these incredibly modern characters and feelings into it, which, combined with a very odd color palette, feels both timeless and contemporary.

"You end up with something that I don't think is ever going to date, which is interesting. They have definitely come up with their own unique look."

"It's unreal, for me, that *Coraline* is now a movie," admits Holly Gaiman, who was the original inspiration for her father's best-selling novel. "I'm now ecstatic that so many people will have the opportunity to follow the tale of Coraline through the movie, and that some of those people will hopefully pick up the book.

In the web living room, all the furniture is made to look like bugs or insects.

"I think the stop-motion medium used by Henry Selick and his team is perfect for telling the story of Coraline, and matches the tone of the original novel so well."

"The movie *Coraline* is a completely marvelous work," agrees her sister Maddy, for whom the original book was finished. "It looks totally wonderful."

"I can guarantee that nobody has seen anything quite like *Coraline*," says the book's creator, Neil Gaiman. "I know that there are plenty of children out there who want to see it. Every single letter I get from every kid who has ever read the book, somewhere in the letter it says:'By the way, I think that *Coraline* would make a really good movie.' Now, I am going to have to write back to all of them saying, 'Well, we've acted on your idea. This was because of you. We made it into a movie.'

"What I really want audiences around the world to take away from the film is terror and joy. If they can take away terror and joy in roughly equal doses, then I will be very happy."

> *Oh—my twitchy witchy girl*
> *I think you are so nice,*
> *I give you bowls of porridge*
> *And I give you bowls of ice*
> *Cream.*
> *I give you lots of kisses,*
> *And I give you lots of hugs,*
> *But I never give you sandwiches*
> *With bugs*
> *In.*

Coraline is happy her real parents are back.

Acknowledgments

The author would especially like to thank for their help and support Neil Gaiman, Henry Selick, Merrilee Heifetz, and Dorothy Lumley; Sarah Durand, Kate Hamill, and Jennifer Brehl (for HarperCollins); Joelle Yudin; Ian McShane, Dave McKean, P. Craig Russell, Stephin Merritt, David Greenspan, Holly Gaiman, Maddy Gaiman, Dario Spinelli, Elise Howard, Galvin Collins, Stacy Ivers, Claire Jennings, and Sarah Odedina; Shelley Midthun, Cindy Rabe, Megan Matousek, and Holly Petersen (for LAIKA); Jennifer Mao, Sasha Silver, David O'Connor, David Bloch, Claire Ripsteen, David Brooks, and Kimberly Lindgren (for NBC Universal/Focus Features); and Niamh Lawlor, Titan Books, Michael Marshall Smith, Claudia Gonson, Maggie Begley, Laura Gross, and Nancy Seltzer.

I would also like to thank Dakota Fanning, Teri Hatcher, Dawn French, Jennifer Saunders, Travis Knight, Georgina Hayns, Chris Butler, Deborah J. Cook, Suzanne Moulton, Amy Adamy, Chris Tootell, Ean McNamara, Bo Henry, Anthony Travis, Elodie Massa-Allen, Joshua Storey, Eric Leighton, Yoji Takenaka, Bill Kispert, and Bill Mechanic.

Art Credits

All still photographs copyright © 2008 LAIKA, Inc.

All behind-the-scenes images, unless otherwise noted, were photographed by Gavin Collins copyright © 2008 LAIKA, Inc.

All illustrations by Tadahiro Uesugi copyright © 2008 LAIKA, Inc.

All original art by Dave McKean, reprinted with permission of Dave McKean.

3   Photograph of Gaiman family at home in England courtesy of the Gaiman family.

4   Photograph of Neil and Holly Gaiman courtesy of the Gaiman family.

5   Pages from Neil Gaiman's handwritten *Coraline* manuscript courtesy of Neil Gaiman.

14   Photograph of Maddy Gaiman courtesy of the Gaiman family.

16   Photograph of Neil Gaiman and Dave McKean by Vanessa Kellas copyright © Jim Henson Company. Courtesy of Dave McKean.

18   Cover of the original British edition of *Coraline* by Neil Gaiman reprinted with permission of Bloomsbury.

20   Photograph of Neil Gaiman and Dave McKean on the set of *Mirrormask* by Mark Spencer copyright © Jim Henson Company. Courtesy of Dave McKean.

20   Cover of the Japanese edition of *Coraline* by Neil Gaiman copyright © Piu Sudo. Cover design by Chigusa Hiraki. Reprinted with permission of Kadokawa Shoten Publishing.

20   Cover of the Korean edition of *Coraline* by Neil Gaiman reprinted with permission of Crown Publishing Company.

20   Cover of the German edition of *Coraline* by Neil Gaiman reprinted with permission of Arena Verlag GmbH.

24–25   Cover and back cover of Subterranean special edition of Neil Gaiman's *Coraline* by Dave McKean. Reprinted with permission of Subterranean Press.

82   Photograph of fabric swatches for the Other Mother by Serena Davidson copyright © 2008 Focus Features LLC. All rights reserved.

82   Photograph of costumes for Coraline's mother by Serena Davidson copyright © 2008 Focus Features LLC. All rights reserved.

137   Photograph of Dakota Fanning performing the voice of Coraline by Sam Emerson copyright © 2008 Focus Features LLC. All rights reserved.

144   Photograph of Teri Hatcher performing the voices of three variations of the Mother by Kelvin Jones copyright © Focus Features LLC. All rights reserved.

161   Photograph of Jennifer Saunders performing the voices of three variations of Miss Spink by Jay Maidment copyright © Focus Features LLC. All rights reserved.

163   Photograph of Dawn French performing the voices of the variations of Miss Forcible by Jay Maidment copyright © 2008 Focus Features LLC. All rights reserved.

171   Photograph of Ian McShane performing the voices of Mr. Bobinsky by Peter Iovino copyright © Focus Features LLC. All rights reserved.

184   Photograph of Keith David performing the voice of the Cat by Kelvin Jones copyright © Focus Features LLC. All rights reserved.

192   Photograph of Robert Bailey, Jr., performing the voice of Wybie by Kelvin Jones copyright © Focus Features LLC. All rights reserved.

193   Photograph of Coraline doll by Serena Davidson copyright © 2008 Focus Features LLC. All rights reserved.

198   The CD art for *Where's Neil When You Need Him?* by Dave McKean reprinted courtesy of Dancing Ferret Discs.

199   Photographs of of Púca Puppets copyright © 2006 Púca Puppets/Jim Berkeley. Photography by Jim Berkeley. Makers: Niamh Lawlor, Fiona Dowling, Maree Kearns, and Maeve Colleary. Puppeteers: Niamh Lawlor, Margot Jones, and Joe Moylan. Directed by Sue Mythen. Soundscape by Slavek Kwi.

200   Poster for the Mittiprickteatern's performance of *Coraline* copyright © Mittiprickteatern/Sarah Englund.

200   Photograph of a scene from the Swedish Mittiprickteatern's *Coraline,* with Ulrika Hansson as Coraline, copyright © Mittiprickteatern/Ragnhild Fridholm.

201   Photographs of scenes from the Swedish Mittiprickteatern's *Coraline,* performed by Magnus Munkesjö as the Other Father, Ulrika Hansson as Coraline, and Eva Welinder as the Other Mother, copyright © Mittiprickteatern/Ragnhild Fridholm.

202   Photograph of Stephin Merritt copyright © Marcelo Krasilcic, reprinted with permission.

204   Cover of the *Coraline* graphic novel, illustrations copyright © P. Craig Russell, published by HarperCollins. Reprinted with permission.

204–205   Excerpts from the *Coraline* graphic novel, illustrations copyright © P. Craig Russell, published by HarperCollins. Reprinted with permission.